Also by Colin Thiele

BLUE FIN
FIRE IN THE STONE

FIGHT AGAINST ALBATROSS TWO

FIGHT AGAINST ALBATROSS TWO

by Colin Thiele

Harper & Row, Publishers
New York, Hagerstown,
San Francisco, London

Library of Congress Catalog Card Number: 75-37104
Trade ISBN 0-06-026098-X
Harpercrest ISBN 0-06-026099-8

FIRST AMERICAN EDITION

Books are seldom created without the help of many people. That was certainly the case with this one.

I therefore wish to thank everyone who gave me time, advice, and information while I was writing *Fight Against Albatross Two*—especially Mrs. Jenny Schultz and the public relations officers of The Australian Mineral Foundation and The Petroleum Information Bureau of Australia.

Above all, I must thank Mr. Bruce Macdonald, without whom I would never have understood the incredible technology of the oil-drilling industry.

Colin Thiele
February 1974

FIGHT AGAINST
ALBATROSS TWO

1

Tina raced down the sand hill. At every stride her feet
sank into the soft sand, so that she had to lollop and
plunge like a colt knee-deep in the sea.

"It's coming!" she yelled. "It's coming."

Below her the faded red roof of her father's boat shed
seemed to lie flat on the beach of the little cove. The
bushes and water sedges at the head of the inlet crowded
right up to it on three sides. In front there was an open
patch of pebbles and sand, above the tidemark, that was
littered with her father's flotsam—old crayfish pots, bits of
rope, broken spars and oars, grapples, rudderposts, oil
drums, and pieces of painted timber from a dozen different
boats. She expected him to be working there with her
brother, Link, but they must have gone inside.

She paused for a second.

"Yoohoo-oo!" she called. "Da-a-ad! Li-i-ink!"

There was no answer, and so she went on hurtling down
the slope. Her feet flung a spray of fine sand ahead of her.
Behind her, the track she was making looked like the wild
plungings of a turtles' chariot race.

"Li-ink," she called again breathlessly, excitedly. "Link,
it's coming!"

Her brother's chunky figure appeared at the door of the
boat shed at last, a mallet and wedge in his hands. He
looked up at her and shouted into the wind.

"How far off?"

Her voice was still thin in the distance, like a sea gull's cry. "Don't know. Come and see."

Link turned toward the open mouth of the shed.

"It's coming, Dad. Tina's spotted it."

Mr. Banks came out and stood beside Link. He cupped his hands to his mouth. "When did you first see it?"

"Just now."

"Still down on the horizon, is it?"

"No, it's big and clear."

"Have you been sleeping on the job, then?"

He said it jokingly, but she snorted out loud all the same. "I've been keeping watch up here for two days. Haven't seen much of you two."

She turned and gazed out to sea for a second. "Come on, hurry up! You can even see it from here now."

They threw down their tools and started to labor up the sand hill toward her. As they did so, the whole world began to grow and spread out below them—the houses, shacks, and shops of the little town, the swamps and un- dulating country stretching inland, the bay curving in behind the headlands and rocky outriders of the coast, and beyond them, the vast southward curve of the open sea.

They were stamping and blowing like dray horses by the time they reached her. She pointed. "See?"

"Wowee!" Link blew out his breath. "It's even big- ger than I thought."

"It's a monster," his father said. "Wait till it comes in closer still."

"How close?"

"Two or three kilometers. That's what they say."

Tina clasped her hands across her chest in the cold wind. "It's frightening," she said. "Like a serpent rising up from the sea."

Her father stood still. He was strangely silent for a while.

"It seems to be coming toward us all by itself—no tugs or anything," said Tina.

"Doesn't need tugs," said Link with the certain knowledge of all fourteen-year-old boys. "Self-powered, semi-submersible, computer-operated."

"Big deal," Tina said.

"Talk like that and maybe it *will* come stomping up the beach and tread the whole town as flat as a flounder."

Their father seemed barely to hear them. "You've got to admit it," he said, half in admiration. "Men are incredible creatures—to create a thing like that."

It was the day *Explorer King* came to Ripple Bay. One of the biggest oil rigs in the world, it moved relentlessly shoreward during the afternoon. As the news of its coming spread through the little settlement, more and more townspeople came streaming up the sand hill to join Tina and Link and Mr. Banks, until it looked as if the whole population of two hundred people was gathering there—whether to welcome it or repulse it was not yet clear. Binoculars and telescopes were rushed up the hill to reveal the monster more clearly still.

"Awful-looking thing," said Mrs. Armstrong from the bakery.

Old Ben Bradshaw elbowed her. "Looks like a mixing machine or a potato masher maybe."

"It'd make paste out of you, Ben Bradshaw. Inferior quality too."

But Otto Holstein from the general store had an eye for trade. "Will be good for business," he said. "Will make plenty moneys come to the place. And that we all want, no?"

Mrs. Potter turned on him suddenly. "No!"

Otto was so surprised that he took a pace back. "But of course."

"No we do not! That Frankenstein out there is one thing Ripple Bay does not need."

She flounced off down the sand hill like an angry nanny about to shake her umbrella in the huge steel face of *Explorer King*.

At four o'clock in the afternoon *Explorer King* slowed down its relentless forward juggernauting and began to maneuver this way and that, as if sniffing out its prey. It was finding the spot, the grid on the map. Three and a half kilometers seaward of Ripple Bay, the computer said. Sector BX147. Zone Permit 643. Spud in on the shelf in sixty meters of water. Drill to a depth of 5000 meters to prove commercial oil and gas. A most important well— Albatross Number Two.

2

After all the excitement of the oil rig's arrival, the next few days were a disappointment. The little town had been waiting for it for months. Rumors had been skipping up and down the coast like will-o'-the-wisps until the oil company finally made its official announcement that the giant rig, *Explorer King*, would be moved from New Guinea to help in the drilling program off the southern coast of Australia. However, even the company couldn't predict the exact speed of the rig's progress, and so Tina Banks had been appointed to the important position of town lookout —to keep watch and to let everybody know the moment the steel lattice of the drilling derrick first reared up above the horizon. She had done her job. But now nothing more seemed to be happening. It was an anticlimax.

"What are they waiting for?" Craypot Potter asked on the second day. "Are they all asleep out there or something?"

"Well what d'you expect them to be doing?" Link asked. "Walking around on top of the water?"

"No, but you'd think there'd be a bit of action."

"Like what?"

"A bit of coming and going for instance."

"Ah, come off it, Craypot," said Len Hook. "It takes time to set up a rig."

5

"Not a semisubmersible," Spinner Turner said. "It just floats."

Helen Rough could not see the point of the argument. "Anyway, even if they were all working like ants out there, you couldn't see anything."

"You could with a telescope. Clear as a daisy."

"That's nice and clear."

Six or seven of them were lounging about the boat shed. Link was supposed to be helping his father weld a cracked propeller shaft, but the welding plant had broken down and Mr. Banks had gone off in a huff all the way to Mount Gambier to have it mended. He'd left Link in charge. The other experts on offshore oil exploration were local schoolmates. Normally, at this time of the morning, they would have been trundling up the road in the old school bus on their way to the Area School at Kangaroo Plains. But it was January—summer holiday time—and school was still four weeks and a million thoughts away.

Four of the group had nicknames which they could only blame their parents for. What other name could a fellow called Craig Potter have than Craypot? Or Bob Turner than Spinner, or Len Hook than Hookie. And of course Helen Rough was called Tommy Ruff. Only Martha Lipchynsky and Jana Bukovitch went without nicknames, probably because the others reckoned they had quite enough to cope with as it was. All their parents, except for Craypot's, made their living from the sea—mainly from crayfish, which they caught during the open season along the rocky coast and shipped to America as frozen lobster tails. Craypot's mother was the postmistress. His father was dead.

6

"It's a nice old size, that rig," Spinner said. "D'you know the length of it?"

"Yes, I measured it yesterday," Craypot said.

Spinner was acidy. "Make a fellow scream with laughter, comedians like you."

"Come on, Mr. Computer," Tommy said good-naturedly. "Let's have the printout!" She was dressed in jeans and the most tattered shirt in Ripple Bay; but it was a carefully stage-managed dilapidation, checked out carefully in front of the mirror each morning to give it a nice natural effect. Tommy hoped Spinner would appreciate a shirt like that, but for the moment he was too full of the oil rig.

"Dad took me for a run around it in the crayboat yesterday." Spinner rolled his eyeballs. "Holy Hopalong!"

Hookie was laconic. "What's that supposed to mean?"

"It's got two submerged hulls—way under the water. You don't know they're there till you get close; then *zap*—you think a pair of submarines are coming at you."

"Why?"

"They're a hundred and fifty meters long."

Craypot scoffed. "A hundred and fifty meters! What a load of crabguts."

Hookie hooted. "That's longer than a running track, sport."

Spinner wouldn't be laughed down. "Exactly. That's what I've been trying to clunk into your thick skulls."

Tommy opened her eyes wide, rather to make Spinner melt than to show any genuine interest in the rig. "Really? Is it really?"

Spinner felt grateful and warmed to her. It was what she'd wanted.

"It absolutely is."

Then, to rattle unbelievers like Craypot and Hookie while their confidence was crumbling, he clouted them with a sockful of statistics: "And the hulls are twenty meters wide and ten meters high. We reckon there's a huge tunnel inside each one, full of engine rooms and pump rooms and piping and whatnot. And from the hulls there are enormous great legs that rise up out of the water to carry the deck—as big as a hockey field it is—and then the derrick sits on top of that."

"And did you measure that too, Einstein?" Craypot was still smarting.

But Spinner was in such full flight that he ignored him. "Sixty meters. And the whole thing is so big it can ride out waves thirty meters high—any sort of storm you like to throw at it."

Hookie was beginning to be interested. "What I want to know is, how do they keep the thing moored in one place? You'd think it would drift about and bust up the drill."

Spinner was equal to such trifles. "Some are kept stationary by automatic motors, and computers and things. But this one's actually moored—like a barge."

Even Craypot was getting interested. "Must be some mooring."

"Ten anchors. Twenty tons each. And ten chains, a thousand meters long and as thick as your leg."

"Each one?"

"Yes, each one."

"Holy Hopalong!"

8

Spinner was feeling very important now. He had them all in his hand. "There are four huge electric motors in each hull—a thousand kilowatts each—and they drive two propellers. Four meters high they are. The whole thing can go like crazy—up to nine knots."

"When it wants to move, you mean?"

"Yes, from one well to the next."

Craypot uncrossed his legs ceremoniously. "I still don't see why they make the thing so big."

"To carry all the junk," Hookie interjected.

"What junk?"

"Equipment," Spinner said airily. "Three thousand tons of gear: piping, cranes, pumps, drilling bits, supplies, mud . . ."

"Mud?"

"Special drilling mud—thousands of barrels of it. For pumping down the drill-hole."

"Crikey."

"And a big helicopter deck, and living quarters for over seventy men, and a geological laboratory, and a radio room, and . . ."

A voice from the boat shed interrupted his flow. "When does the next lucky tour start? Tickets from Turner's tourist desk, fifty cents."

It was Link.

He put his head out of the boat shed door and gave them a raspberry with his thumb. "Why don't you bludgers go and do some work for a change. The country needs you."

They broke up slowly. Tommy Rough persuaded Spinner to go looking for driftwood where there wasn't any, so that she could have him to herself, and the others went up into the town to wait for something to happen. Mr. Banks returned from Mount Gambier soon afterward and kept Link busy in the workshop for most of the day, so they didn't know whether anything did happen or not.

Back at home Tina wasn't much better off than her brother. She was helping her Aunt Jessica with the housework. First the sweeping and dusting, then the ironing, then cutting apricots for jam. She sat on the floor of the front verandah overlooking the bay, arranged her spindly legs around the bowl of fruit, and sliced away silently and steadily—for all the world like a praying mantis in a print dress. Every fifth or sixth slice she popped into her mouth.

"Not too much munching out there," her aunt called from inside the house. "You should be whistling while you work."

Tina hastily swallowed the piece she had in her mouth and called back, "I don't feel in a whistling mood."

"Be good for you all the same. Especially for your stomach. Spare it from getting the gripes later on."

Tina laughed. She liked her aunt in a mother-sister kind of way. She and Link called her Jesse James, or Six-Gun for short. She was good fun when she was well, which wasn't all that often. But then she had to put up with Link, Tina, and their father, and act as cook, housekeeper, nurse, mother, sister, bank manager, and overseer most of the time, and that wasn't easy.

For Tina's real mother was dead. Aunt Jessica was an unmarried sister—a much older one—who had always suffered from asthma or hay fever or allergies of one sort or another. When Tina's mother had been drowned in a tragic accident about six years before, Auntie Jessica had come down to the South Coast to try to improve her health and look after her brother-in-law's household at the same time. She had stayed on ever since.

Tina went on gravely slicing her apricots. Every now and then she looked up from the bowl and gazed out over the sea. It was peaceful: just a gentle breeze from the south; the blue water rucked up into little waves; the sea gulls hanging on the air like small white kites held on invisible strings. Yet somehow the place was different now —different from what it had always been. She could feel it in her bones. And the reason was out there beyond the bay, as plain as a mountain. Halfway to the horizon it heaved up huge and squat like the deck of an aircraft carrier, with the poppet-head of a mine shaft rearing higher above it still. *Explorer King!*

Tina put down her knife and sat watching the rig for a long time. She was trying to work out the reason for her feelings about it. Not that it was ugly, exactly. Even from this distance the booms of the cranes and the jutting helicopter deck gave it a modern angular look. Like a signaling station semaphoring with arms of steel lacework.

No, it was what it stood for that was the important thing. It was a sign, a symbol of everything that was foreign to Ripple Bay, of freeways and steel jungles and jet power and smog—and war. It just didn't go with white water, or crayfish that were crawling about in rocky grottoes, or ancient untouched coastlines, or clean winds over the headlands, or bright sand in little inlets. It didn't fit in. It was

11

black where the breakers were white; it was greasy where things were clean; it was brash where life was gentle; it was fire where the world was water.

Tina puckered up her brow and looked away. It wasn't the first time in her twelve-year-old life that she had felt the dark currents of change swirling around her. She could still remember the death of her mother clearly and terribly—the whispers in the town about a woman swept away in a flooded channel while she was trying to rescue a schoolchild, the gatherings of police and search parties, the calls for her father, the numbing realization that it was her own mother they were talking about, the news of the body being found, and the strange emptiness of the house without a mother to get the tea or wash the dishes. Even the arrival of Aunt Jessica was nothing but further change. She was still "Miss James" to the people of the town, and her tongue was so proper at first that it called out "Christina" and "Lincoln" unbelievably from the kitchen, whenever dinner was ready. However, time had flowed over all that, and what had been raw and new slowly became normal and expected. The neighbors, when they thought she wasn't listening, called it "healing the wound." But it had left a scar just the same.

Tina finished the last apricot and swished her fingers in the rinse water. Then she stood up, bent like an old woman, and stretched her back.

"Need a walking stick, Granny?"

Aunt Jessica was standing behind her. She stooped to help pick up the bowls and dishes and stood gazing out at the sea.

"Ooh, I hate that thing," she said suddenly. "Gives me

the creeps. Looks like a shipwreck, or a sunken factory or something. Like the bombed-out wreckage in Darwin Harbor during the war."

Tina paused and looked back as she was about to go inside. She hadn't really thought of the rig as a shipwreck, even though her father said half of it was underwater. At least that idea fitted in with the place. There'd been hundreds of wrecks and drownings up and down the coast—from the *Admella* on Carpenter's Rocks to the *Maria* on the beach by the Coorong.

"Come in and set the table," Aunt Jessica said. "Lincoln and your father will be up for lunch in a minute."

Tina didn't get out of the house until late in the afternoon. Then she ran briskly down the road past the single row of shops—past Mrs. Armstrong's bakery, old Otto Holstein's general store, and Rossi's deli; past the post office and community hall; past the red-roofed Commercial Hotel with its enclosed second-story balcony looking out over the sea; past Bradshaw's garage to the sandy tussock country at the head of the inlet, where her father's boat shed hunched itself against the sand hills like a half-buried anteater. She went inside quickly, lifted up the lid of the old freezer her father kept there for bait and leftovers, took out three or four fish, and went on around the sand hills toward the headland beyond.

Three houses stood near the headland in somber solitude. Mrs. Potter, the postmistress, lived in one of them with Craypot and his older sister. Next to this was a beach house owned by someone in Adelaide. It stood empty for half the year, and then suddenly burst at the seams over-

night with a great dollop of awful people from the city.
Next to that again was a solid old cottage with a pointed
picket fence that was owned by a Mr. Hackett. He was
a queer fish, everyone said. Some thought he was retired,
and some said that he wrote important books and papers
for the university, and some were sure he was a spy. Tina
liked him.

He was leaning against the gate smoking his pipe as she
hurried past.

"Hullo, Tina," he called cheerfully. "Off to feed Piglet?"

"Yes, Mr. Hackett."

"Didn't see you last night."

"I was running late; we'd been watching the oil rig."

"Oh, that. It's caused a bit of a stir in the town."

"Yes."

"And more to come, I should think."

"I guess so."

He sighed. "Oh well, that's progress, they say."

She was in a hurry, but she felt she should wait just a
moment or two to be polite.

"Spinner says it's one of the biggest in the world."

"Is that so? And who's Spinner?"

"Bob Turner. Craypot's friend."

"I see."

Mr. Hackett pursed his lips and blew out a thin stream
of white pipe smoke. Suddenly he seemed to make a decision and swung open the picket gate.

"I think I'll come with you tonight—if you don't mind.
To visit Piglet."

She would really have preferred to have gone on alone, because she could climb down the rocks so much more quickly on her own, but she didn't want to seem rude.

"You haven't seen him for a while."

"Two weeks at least, I should think. How is he?"

"Very well. He's fattened up during the summer."

They walked on briskly to the lip of the cliffs a little farther on. Just inside the arc of the headland, the hard capping had broken away in a great tumbling mass of rock, and it was possible to pick a path to the pebbly beach below. Halfway down, a shelf ran off to the right where the cliffs were pocked with holes, and caves, and long fissures winding in every direction.

Tina and Mr. Hackett made their way along the shelf to a double cave that looked like an owl's skull. There they stopped, and Tina called out gently, "Piglet! Come on, Piglet. Special treat."

There was a moment's silence, followed by a rustling, slapping sound, and then a little figure suddenly popped out in front of them. They both bent forward.

"Hullo, Piglet."

"Good evening, Piglet."

It was a small Australian penguin called a fairy penguin. It stood in front of its burrow for a minute looking at them, and then waddled forward hastily with its flippers held out—like a little child asking to be picked up. It was almost as big as a walking baby.

"A treat, Piglet," Tina said, opening her parcel. "Fish."

She held up a pilchard and popped it headfirst into the penguin's open bill. There it was waggled and flung about from side to side for a second before disappearing into Piglet's gullet.

"Good boy. More?" Tina held up another pilchard. "Come on. Nice?" Another waggle and flurry and the second fish was gone too.

"He likes pilchards," Mr. Hackett said.

"Loves them. When he was hurt, he lived on nothing else. He would have died, otherwise."

She bent forward on her knees and put out her hand. After a minute's hesitation, the little penguin let her rub his throat and tickle the back of his neck.

"Good boy, Piglet. Oh, you are getting fat and strong, aren't you?" She rummaged in her parcel.

"One left. Want it?" Piglet's bill was already wide open. "Greedy guts."

In went the fish, jostled and shaken, and was gone. "You're a real piglet."

Mr. Hackett picked up the paper wrapping. "Is that why he got his name?"

"Yes. We did it for fun. When we found him lying on the beach after the big storm the winter before last, we thought he was dead. He nearly was. But we took him home and kept him warm and snug for a while, and he got better. Before long he was eating so many fish that Dad complained. He and Link could hardly keep up the supply. So we called him Piglet."

"He's been tame ever since?"

"Tame as a pet."

"But you turned him loose again when he was better."

"Dad made us. He said fairy penguins were born free."

"He was right, you know." Mr. Hackett got up creakily to his feet. "And it's better this way, Tina. See, you've got a real friend for life."

"I guess. He always comes when I call him—if he's at home, that is." She gave the little penguin a parting hug. "See you, Piglet."

The bird stood up on his toes and flapped his flippers in a flurry of excitement. Even in the half-light of evening the soft blue color of his back stood out clearly all the way down to his stubby tail. His pale fleshy feet looked pink against the dark rocks, and his throat and chest shone with whiteness.

"Oh you are a nice clean fellow," Tina said. "I'm very proud of you." She turned to Mr. Hackett. "He uses the best soap powder, you know."

Mr. Hackett laughed. "Sees it advertised on TV, I expect." They both waved. "Good-bye, Piglet. See you next time!"

Piglet did not turn and go back into his burrow. Instead he stayed at the entrance, watching them climb all the way back up the rocks.

"Beautiful creatures," Mr. Hackett said, panting and wheezing out the words between breaths. "Unfortunately . . . they're getting . . . scarce. Killed off. Farmers, dogs, ferrets, cats . . . even cars. They run over them on the roads. Like everything else. . . . It's men that are the trouble. . . ."

"I wish people would leave them alone," Tina said. "They only lay two eggs at a time. And they take forty days to hatch. A lot get broken."

17

Mr. Hackett kicked a loose stone angrily and sent it skidding up the track. "I know. People with sticks, poking and prodding. Visitors. Tourists." They had reached the flat land beyond the cliffs and were approaching the picket fence in front of Mr. Hackett's cottage. "Thank you, Tina," he said. "I always enjoy meeting Piglet."

"That's all right. I think he's getting to know you now."

"I must remember to keep some pilchards fresh, especially for him."

"He'd love you then," she said laughingly. She looked around at the gathering darkness. "I've got to run. It's late."

"Good-bye, Tina. And thank you again."

"Good-bye, Mr. Hackett."

As she ran down past the boat shed she caught up with Link and her father on their way home to tea. All three of them trudged up the slope. Suddenly some red lights winked on angrily out at sea, followed by two brilliant orange arc lamps that threw up a distant glow.

"They've started the big diesels, by the look of it," Link said. "Won't be long now."

Tina looked over toward the lights. It was hard to imagine sixty or seventy men toiling out there across the water. "Have they started drilling yet?"

Mr. Banks was getting ahead of them up the road. "Any minute, I'd say."

"But they don't drill at night, do they?" Tina asked.

Her father laughed dryly. "Right around the clock, twenty-four hours a day, seven days a week."

"What, even on Sundays?"

Link hooted. "Wakey, wakey," he said. "Oil rigs don't go to bed, and they're not in the habit of going to church either."

They reached the front verandah of the house and looked back for the last time. The red lights were still there. To Tina they were not signals of warning and safety. They were symbols of danger, the red eyes of menace.

3

Wednesday was a great day for Tina and Link. It was the day of the test run for old *Titan*.

Their father had bought her for fifty dollars—a beat-up harbor-scarred old Glasgow tug that had already been an antique when she started her workhorse job in Port Melbourne before the First World War. All the people of Ripple Bay had nearly fallen out of their Sunday deck chairs in amazement at the sight of a bashed-up, hundred-year-old floating iron dump heading into the anchorage. It had flopped along like a water-logged duck. Its whole superstructure—deck, bow, funnel, wheelhouse, wireless mast, and hatch—was white and pungent with the messages of shags and sea gulls.

But that didn't worry Mr. Banks or his three friends who had helped to sail her home. He had stood proudly in the wheelhouse, blowing the foghorn and waving his cap through the broken glass pane beside him to all the people who had come streaming down to the jetty to see him tie up.

"Oldest tug in Australia," he had shouted. "Going to be part of our nautical museum."

It was a dream he'd always had—the museum. He wanted to gather together all the relics from a hundred wrecks, old treasures that now lay scattered about in homes and houseyards all over southeastern Australia. Some people laughed at him. "Look, Dave," old Grandpa Fletcher had said with a twinkle, "your own boat shed is a museum as it is. Just put it in a big glass case and people would come hundreds of miles to see it. Especially with you inside it."

Mr. Banks had chuckled at that. "Naturally," he said. "I'm descended from Sir Joseph Banks. He was another great sailor who kept a museum."

And so old *Titan* was saved for the Ripple Bay Historical Society. But she was not to be chocked up on shore like a load of junk till she fell to pieces. She was to be a living museum, kept in apple-pie order, ready to toot about with a load of townspeople on any Sunday they liked. Link and Tina helped restore her.

Their father was very proud of them, not only because they had worked hard themselves, but because they had brought along dozens of their school friends to help. Link worked on the Tom Sawyer principle—especially with fellows like Craypot and Spinner who were a bit reluctant at first.

"It's incredible the way you find things hidden on the old girl," Link would remark to his friends. "Inscriptions and signs and brand names and things. But you can't see 'em till you've scraped off the muck and polished up the metal." He would pause. "Course it's very skilled work; not everyone can do it."

"Give us a go, Link."

"I don't know, Craypot. I reckon Dad'd go acidy if he found out."

"Ah, come on, Link."

"Well, if you keep it to yourselves."

Link used the same ploy with the woodwork. The girls were better at it than the boys.

And so, day by day and centimeter by centimeter, old *Titan* had been restored. Mr. Banks worked on the engine, while his free labor did the decks and the hull. Then came a coat of paint, and inspection for seaworthiness, and she was ready for her sea trials—off Ripple Bay.

It was a beautiful day. All the helpers were invited on board as part of their reward, because the Tom Sawyer privilege had started to wear a bit thin toward the end, and Link wanted to buck them up. Terry Armstrong from the garage came too, to act as engineman, and big Mostyn Mankovitz, who had a chest like a barrel and thighs like gum-tree trunks. Everyone applauded when he came aboard, because they said that if the tug broke down he could climb over the side and carry her back on his shoulders. And at the last minute Mr. Hackett came sauntering along, sucking at his bent pipe; and, seeing the holiday happiness spread all over the old ship like a grin, he called out to Mr. Banks, "Dave, do you mind if I beg a passage too?"

"Hop on. Everyone's welcome."

"Thanks. Jolly good of you."

"Thank the old lady."

"Who?" Mr. Hackett looked about as if searching for Aunt Jessica.

"Old *Titan*."

Mr. Hackett relaxed. "Oh. Oh, I see." He paused while

he untangled his fingers from the grip of his pipe. "Should be called *Titaness*, shouldn't she—if she's a lady?"

"Not this old girl. She'd have an explosion in her pipes at a name like that."

He blew the foghorn. "All aboard." He was wearing a greatcoat over his overalls, and a sou'wester on his head.

"Every bit a captain, if I may say so," said Mr. Hackett.

Mr. Banks thrust his head out of the wheelhouse. "Prepare to cast off," he yelled. "Ready engine room. Slow speed ahead."

They began to edge away from the jetty in a nice flurry of foam from the screw. Everyone hooted and yelled. Mr. Banks raised his hand imperiously. "Only one thing we didn't do," he said. "We forgot to re-christen her with champagne."

"The spray will do it better," big Mostyn said. "She likes that." And she did.

Out in the open water old *Titan* charged all seas with the same bull-butting solidity. She rose heavily on one wave and flopped ungracefully into the following trough. Then she spent too long wallowing down there to rise in time for the next wave, and so she just put her heavy bow straight into it and flung water and spray in all directions. The passengers shrieked and retreated to the stern.

"A new kind of submarine," said Craypot grumpily. "Why didn't you warn me—I would have worn my snorkel."

Link was terse. "You're always wearing it—with a conk like yours."

But most of the others reveled in the trip. "See, it's an underwater museum," Spinner said.

"Davy Jones has got hundreds of 'em," Craypot answered. "Remind me to tell you about him."

They were all so busy milling about and wiping spray from their eyes that they didn't really notice *Explorer King* until they were almost upon it. Then, suddenly, its enormous bulk seemed to rear right in front of them, heaving up gigantically and towering over them like a colossus. In an instant *Titan* seemed to shrink to the size of a water beetle. Silence fell on everyone; laughter was quenched, jokes stifled. In the hush they could hear the slap of the waves against the tug's plates and the hiss of the bow wave in surges like escaping steam. The air seemed to be cold around their shoulders. Then Link spoke quietly. "Wowee! Just look at it."

Spinner gazed unbelievingly. "Holy Hopalong!"

The uprights of the giant rig looked for all the world like huge legs going down far under the water to join two feet as big as barges.

"How would you like a thing like that to come walking into your bedroom on a dark night?" Hookie said.

Tina was still awestruck. "I'd die!"

"You could fit your whole house on its little toenail."

"And the Community Hall in its heel."

They were still gawking and commenting when a voice shouted at them from a loudspeaker. "Hi there! Get that old tosspot out of here."

Tina was genuinely startled. "My gosh," she said, "the thing can talk!"

24

Link growled. "It's probably been watching us with infrared eyes."

The voice broke out again. "You should know better than to bring that thing so close." It had an American accent and seemed annoyed. "There's a proclaimed safety zone. A hundred meters all around."

"Bully for you," Link shouted out rudely. But his voice was lost in the wind and the surge.

"He's a sensitive monster," Mr. Banks said wryly, swinging the wheel hard over. "Can't even stand visitors."

Old *Titan* clattered off in a wide arc, leaving the foam of its wake breaking and tossing among the huge support columns of *Explorer King*. As she did so, the passengers had a clear view of the whole rig—the wide deck, the booms of the cranes, the overhanging helicopter pad, the tapering tower of the derrick.

"Look!" Tina suddenly shouted excitedly, pointing up at the deck. "Look at the men. They're as tiny as thumbs."

It was true. About a dozen men were busy with piping and other drilling gear. Sometimes they disappeared from sight in the center of the rig somewhere, but now and again they came close to the edges of the platform. It was like watching the busy life of midgets ten centimeters high, engrossed in their own affairs.

"Why do they use such little men?" Craypot asked Tommy Rough with a crooked grin.

But Tommy was curt. "So they can drop 'em down the hole when the drill gets stuck—like chimney sweeps." *Titan* was moving away at a great rate now, running before the breeze. The whole rig seemed to be shrinking in

25

perspective. Tommy pointed back at the men. "And they're getting smaller all the time," she said to Craypot. "Soon you won't be able to see them at all. They're a new kind of man—called Disappearing Digger. They feed them on special pills." She looked at Craypot quizzically. "You wouldn't like to try some, I s'pose?"

"Try what?"

"Some disappearing pills."

"Very funny," said Craypot testily. He moved toward the bow, preferring the sting of the spray to Tommy's tongue.

Halfway back to the jetty, Mr. Banks handed the wheel over to Link, while he went back to talk to Terry Armstrong about the engine. Link's chest expanded so much that it stretched the stitches of his pullover. All the others looked at him enviously, and even big Mr. Mankovitz clicked his heels, saluted, and shouted, *"Heil, Herr Kapitän!"*

Link liked his father. They were always pottering about together in the boat shed, building dinghies for the other fishermen, slipping and painting crayboats, and repairing masts, keels, rudders, winches, and even oars. As soon as he was old enough to leave school—within a year or so—he was going to join his father full time. They might even become Banks and Son, Boatbuilders. His bond with his father had made it easier for Link when his mother had been drowned, while poor Tina had had to cope with the empty house and Aunt Jessica. And he was strong. He looked a bit tubby to an outsider, with his big chest and round face, but everyone at Ripple Bay knew that he had his father's solid shoulders. He could haul up craypots like a man, or throw boxes full of fish from the boat onto the jetty.

Tina wasn't so lucky. She was more lanky, and less sure of herself than Link. And she had freckles—so thick that it looked as if tapioca pudding had been dried out all over her cheeks. Aunt Jessica said it was because she was always outside in the sun and wind instead of doing the housework indoors; which was unkind, because Tina actually helped in the house a lot, even though she preferred to be down in the boat shed with Link or romping over the sand hills or clambering along the rocky coast in search of Piglet and the other fairy penguins.

So it was no wonder, with Link at the wheel of old *Titan*, that Tina was standing in the bows holding on to the anchor stanchion—the spume sweeping over her in bursts and the wind like marble against her freckled cheeks. It wasn't just that she liked doing things like that. It was a gesture, a position she was adopting deliberately. Like running up a flag. The message was quite clear too. "I'm Tina," it said, "and I'm nobody else. And even if I'm not as lucky as Link, because he's got Dad to himself all day and I've only got Aunt Jessie; and even if the boys don't make a fuss of me, because I'm skinny and plastered with freckles; and even if I'm no great shakes at school and Miss Lane thinks I'm a bit of a twit—well, I'm still Tina Banks and I'm Mum's daughter. She was a powerhouse in the district when she was alive—a leader of women, *and* of men too. She wouldn't have lost her life if she hadn't been diving into a flooded channel as wide as a river to try to save a little girl. Mum had spunk, and so have I."

"Look at the figurehead we've got," Spinner yelled. "She's the Lady Titan."

"She's ugly enough," Craypot said. He shouted at Tina. "You're supposed to lie down and butt your head through the waves."

Tina stood stolidly in the bows and said nothing.

Her silence nettled Craypot; he started to get vindictive. "It might improve your complexion."

Tommy Rough knew how much a joke like that would hurt Tina. She turned on him. "Oh, go and bag your head, Craypot; the spray running off you is starting to pollute the sea."

The jetty was beginning to loom up ahead and Link knew it was time to cut back speed. His father was still busy with Terry Armstrong.

Link was in a quandary. He wasn't sure that he could berth *Titan* on his own, although he'd handled crayboats and cutters often enough. On the other hand his pride would never allow him to call his father and ask him to take over. Not with twenty of his grinning classmates watching him. He had to make a quick decision.

"Half speed ahead," he called. And then, more urgently when there was no response, "Half ahead, half ahead."

Terry Armstrong heard the faint note of alarm in Link's voice and hastily cut back the engine. But *Titan* had too much way. She was like a long-rested war horse with the bit between her teeth. The jetty was rushing nearer at a frightening rate. Tina, in the bows, turned uneasily and looked at Link.

"Dead slow! Dead slow!" Link yelled. But the cumbersome old tug was a long time responding. He could sense her weight and was appalled at her relentless, juggernauting onrush—not like a light crayboat that was almost as maneuverable as a dinghy. The jetty was desperately close now. Link looked at it wide-eyed. Within seconds he would be reaching the point of no return. Either he had to heave the wheel around hard to starboard and take *Titan* around in a circle for a second try, or he had to back his belief that he could stop her in time. He glanced quickly at the coast and the curve of the little bay. There wasn't really room for her to complete a circle; and running her aground or piling her into the rocks would be worse than demolishing the jetty. It would wreck her for good.

Link made his decision. As he did so he was vaguely aware of a sense of resentment against his father for not coming to his aid long before this. What he didn't realize was that the whole emergency had developed in thirty or forty seconds; it seemed more like ten or fifteen minutes.

"Astern!" he yelled shrilly. "Full speed astern."

The jetty was only twenty meters off.

"Astern! Astern!"

His father came leaping up to the wheelhouse, shouting back at Terry as he came, "Astern Terry! Hard! Hard!"

Ten meters. The screw took an agonizing age to respond.

Seven meters. At last she was gripping. The sea began to boil under the stern. Five meters. Tina turned and jumped back from the bows, her face tense with alarm, her eyes on Link. "Look out, Link! You'll hit! You're going to hit."

Three meters. Old *Titan*'s screw was roaring now, foam belching up around it like fountains of detergent. They could feel her digging in her heels—like a horse rider skidding before a crash. Mr. Banks grabbed his son's shoulders. "Give me the wheel, Link."

One meter. She was heaving back prodigiously, checking herself more and more with every instant. But it wasn't enough.

"Hang on, everyone!" Tina and her father yelled simultaneously.

He swung the wheel sharply to starboard as they were about to strike, and the bow swung along the edge of the decking, fending off the impact in a sideswipe. There was a jolt and a splintering of hardwood timber as a couple of heavy bearers were carried away. Ahead of them was a rickety set of old steps that led down steeply from the deck of the jetty to the water. *Titan* still had a bit of way left. Like a slow old bull goring lazily at a wood heap, she put her bow against the steps and reared upward on the swelling waves of her own making. There was a hideous grinding, a tearing of wood and metal rails, and the whole set of steps disintegrated into useless junk. *Titan* went on for a meter farther, struck one of the main piles with a jolt strong enough to send Craypot and Tommy Rough forward on their knees, and came to rest at last, rocking as gently as a petal in a pond.

"By Jimminy!" old Mostyn Mankovitz said, goggle-eyed. "That was nearly good-bye jetty, no? I think one time we all finish up in the main street by the pub."

Tommy Rough ignored the helping hand Craypot half extended to help her up. "I'm all right," she said, embarrassed at being the only girl who had fallen over.

"Having a bit of trouble keeping your feet, are you, Craypot?" Spinner asked. "Haven't been drinking, have you?"

Craypot pretended to dust down his jeans. "Blooming learner drivers," he said, glaring at Link in the wheel-house. "Lucky we didn't cut the jetty in two."

Mr. Hackett was lighting his pipe ceremoniously with a great show of unconcern. "Oh well, we've argued about replacing those steps for years because they were danger-ous. Now old *Titan* has got rid of them at least. Done us a good turn, really."

Several people laughed. Link came out of the wheel-house red-faced and confused. He was grateful to Mr. Hackett for the laughter, because it took the tension out of the air; and he was even more grateful for his father's quick comment, "Never mind, son. No real harm done." But he'd learned one thing—the heavier the ship, the more momentum she carried with her. It was a lesson to remember.

When they were all walking home an hour or two later, after tying up old *Titan* and clearing up some of the mess, Tina moved up close to Link.

"Sorry Link," she said, "for yelling at you—just before she hit the jetty."

"Not to worry; there was good reason."

"I should have known better all the same. Must have made you feel a goat. I know what it's like."

Link gave her a strange look. "Yes," he said.

And because they understood one another, they walked home the rest of the way in silence.

31

4

The news of *Titan*'s exploit flowed through the district
like a fast tide. It swept up the main street in a flood of
comment and excitement, swirled about in the pub and
general store, where it picked up a mixed debris of exag-
geration, distortion, and rumor, eddied endlessly in Mrs.
Potter's post office until it was muddy and polluted, and
finally rushed out over the wide incredulous countryside.

"And to think that my Craig was actually on it," Mrs.
Potter cried as she gazed wide-eyed at her customers. She
gave her voice a trembling note to suggest cataclysms, sea
serpents, and waterspouts. "It was a miracle he wasn't
killed, the way they were all hurled down onto the deck.
Such a terrible crash, you see. It shook the whole town;
even up here I felt the counter shake."

"Who was at the wheel, for goodness' sake?"

"Young Lincoln."

"Who?"

"Lincoln. Dave Banks's boy."

"Oh, Link."

"Yes. Too big for his boots. He's only fourteen. There'll
be an inquiry over this—half the jetty smashed and all. It's
a miracle that someone wasn't killed."

But the town didn't really have time to taste the story
properly. For if Wednesday had been a day of news and

excitement, it was nothing compared with Thursday—the first day of the oilmen's invasion, and the second jetty crash within twenty-four hours. It started when Mario Bukovitch, John Leckie, and a fleet of their colleagues came in fuming from the crayfishing grounds. Mario was so red-hot that it was surprising the mooring ropes didn't scorch when he breathed on them.

"I cut their throats," he raged dramatically. "They say once more 'get outa here, keep clear outa here!' I blow them all up. I get my gelignite out."

The crayboats had had a good run and were all clustered around the jetty, unloading. Every berth was taken and three or four boats were moored two abreast—the crew of the outer one having right of transit across the inner one.

"For twenty years, nearly, I am coming in and outa this bay," Mario grizzled on, "and nobody's saying you don't go this way, you gotta go that way. I been here all that time, and so is John, and Emanuel, and Dave, and all these boys, and nobody's ever been saying to them get outa here, keep offa here. The sea, she is free. Till now."

It was obvious that old *Titan* hadn't been the only local vessel warned off by the loudspeaker on *Explorer King*. Most of the fishing fleet seemed to have been given the same treatment.

But the real explosion was still to come. Shortly before noon the sound of powerful engines could be heard approaching Ripple Bay. Everybody looked up. It was a tender from the oil company—a big bull-shouldered vessel that looked like a military landing barge. It crashed through the waves in a fury of spray and came roaring into the bay. The men who were working on the jetty left their jobs and stood watching. Some of the crayboats had finished unloading and had put out to sea again, but most of them were still tied to their moorings. Link and his father were getting ready to take John Leckie's boat *Dolphin* around to the slip to fix a broken rudder pin, and were standing near the engine well as the tender approached.

Mario Bukovitch voiced everyone's uneasiness. "What is this? More troubles coming."

"Ugly brute of a thing," Link said. "You half expect a couple of gunports to open up and howitzers or recoilless cannons to pop out."

Mr. Banks laughed sourly. "Mario would be ready for them," he said. "He'd fire words at them like bullets, in a dozen different languages."

The tender's engines revved violently as the helmsman put them into reverse to check his speed. The din of their power was deafening; it roared over the men on the jetty, filled the bay, and went thundering out over the reefs and headlands beyond. Seabirds along the coast rose shrieking and townspeople ran to their windows. The onrushing bow wave from the tender swept along under the jetty, rocking and pitching the crayboats like cockleshells. It nearly upended Link over the side, and even John Leckie had to grab hastily at a hatch cover for support. No sooner had the wave surged past than the maelstrom from the reversing screws struck the boats. The water boiled and eddied in every direction at once, and the crews could do

34

nothing but hang on till the worst of the turbulence was over.

"Crazy galoots," John Leckie said angrily.

"Putting on a show for the locals," Mr. Banks said.

The tender came inching toward the jetty. There wasn't room for its whole length anywhere, so the helmsman was trying to do the best he could by getting half of it alongside, leaving the rest jutting out into the bay. It was ticklish work, but he did it well. Slowly the iron bulk slid into place, gently grazing the decking. Stylish seamanship.

And then, at the last minute, disaster! Anxious to squeeze the last centimeter out of the space for his mooring, he overshot the distance and struck the crayboat that was facing him. The blunt steel bow of the tender snapped off the bowsprit and then, swinging wide, rode harshly down the boat's side for a meter or so, leaving a wide scar on the clean white paint. The boat belonged to Mario Bukovitch.

It took Mario a second or two to comprehend what had happened. He stood staring at the damage with a ludicrous look of disbelief on his face, his mouth open and his sock cap pushed so far back on his head that the pom-pom on the end hung down to the small of his back like a girl's overgrown ponytail. Then all hell broke loose.

"You dirty hog-pigs," Mario yelled. "Look what you done. You smash my boat."

Several crewmen holding mooring lines from the tender leaped onto the jetty to secure her. Mario rushed at them like a blast from a furnace door. He gave the first one an enormous shove that sent him skidding along the deck, still holding the rope and wearing an expression of mild

35

amazement. The second one turned just in time to see Mario descending on him like lava from Mount Etna, gave a wild yell of terror, and leaped back onto the tender again.

"You better stay there," Mario shouted. "Santa Maria, I kill you!"

The man he had knocked down had scrambled to his feet and hastily wound the line around a bollard so that at least his vessel was held from drifting. Mario lunged at him again and drove him back on board too.

"You better not get off here," Mario yelled, patrolling up and down the jetty like a lion to prevent anyone from landing. "You better not, or I tear you up." He had a great reputation for being able to tear telephone directories in two with his bare hands, and instinctively put up his fists and gave them a savage twist in demonstration. "I tear you up the middle."

Suddenly a tall man stepped forward from the rear of the tender and stood on the deck plates near the edge of the jetty. He was strong and straight, with a sun-browned face and crinkles around his eyes. He was wearing a khaki shirt and trousers, and a cap like an officer's. He almost looked like a wartime navy man.

"What's the trouble?" he asked in an American voice. "No need to get hot under the collar."

Mario was flabbergasted at such a stupid question. "What'sa trouble!" he cried, outraged. "You'sa trouble! First you say I can no sail where I want, and now you smash my boat."

"I'm sorry," said the man.

"Sorry!" Mario exploded in disbelief. "You stick sorry up your jumper. You pay!"

"Okay! Okay! We'll pay for the damage."

"That's right! You pay, you pay."

"It's not serious."

"Huh!" Mario leaped forward, pointing furiously at the bow of his boat. "No serious! Is serious I can no go fishing today. Is serious my pots fulla crayfish and I no come."

"Well, we'll pay compensation."

"What's this compensation, what's this?" Mario felt he was being given a double deal in some way he didn't understand, so he cut through all the talk with a clear ultimatum: "This morning you tell me clear outa here, no? Now I tell you—you clear outa here too."

By now most of the other fishermen had gathered on the jetty. Link and his father followed John Leckie up, and presently some of the townspeople came flocking around too. The big man saw the gathering crowd and sensed even greater trouble. He looked the kind of fellow who had had experience with trouble in all sorts of places around the world, and it was obviously in the interests of the oil company to avoid clashes with local people wherever possible. Perhaps the sight of big Mostyn Mankovitz coming up the causeway toward the jetty like a walking gum tree decided the issue. At any rate the oilman drew himself up impressively and called out in a loud voice, "Is there anyone here who's got a slip or a workshop?"

There was a moment's silence and then Mr. Banks spoke up. "I've got both."

"Good," the tall man said. "How long will it take you to fix this guy's crayboat?"

"Three or four hours."

"Then I'll tell you what. You fix it by three o'clock and

I'll pay you what it costs, and throw in fifty dollars extra." There was another pause. "What d'you say?"

Link looked at his father, who seemed to be considering things very carefully. "Sorry," he said at last, "another job has priority."

The oilman was disappointed. "What job?"

"John Leckie's rudder pin." Link's father hesitated again. "But I reckon I could finish them both by four o'clock."

"Good. You've got yourself a contract." The visitor turned to Mario, who had been glowering like a volcano while all this was going on. "Your boat'll be fixed today. And again I apologize."

There was a murmur among the listeners which suggested satisfaction, much to Mario's disgust. He went off into another tirade, but there was less sympathy for him now. Some of the fishermen broke off and went on with their work, and the townspeople began drifting back up the street. Mario turned his attention to Mr. Banks. "You be quick, Dave. Three o'clock."

"Four o'clock, Mario."

"Half past three."

"Four."

"*Diàvolo!*" Mario spat out the word and flounced off.

Mostyn Mankovitz shook with laughter, like a pudding as big as a bathtub. *"Donner und blitzen,"* he roared jovially, mimicking Mario.

As Link and Mr. Banks went back to the *Dolphin* with John Leckie, Link glanced guardedly at his father. He wondered whether the offer to help the oilmen out of their

38

difficulty had been a wise move, especially when the general mood of the town was running strongly against the rig. But he needn't have worried. There was no fairer man in Ripple Bay than Dave Banks, and everyone knew it.

They were so busy for the next few hours that Link didn't know how quickly the time passed. They had repaired the *Dolphin*'s rudder and were busy on Mario's *Corfu*—Link sanding down and painting the scar, his father fitting a new bowsprit—when the tall oilman suddenly appeared again. They had winched the boat halfway up the slip and were making good progress. "How's she coming?" he asked jovially.

Mr. Banks didn't pause in his work. "Pretty right."

"Will you make it on time—for our Adriatic friend?"

"Just about."

The tall man went over and stood near the bow. His head was almost on a level with Mr. Banks's. "I want to say how much I appreciate this," he said warmly. "It's the company's policy to avoid trouble if it can—and you've helped a lot." He hesitated, as if debating about the next sentence. "We could really have started off on the wrong foot, all because of that young fool helmsman."

Mr. Banks looked up at last. "He's not the first one to overshoot the mark," he said, glancing wryly at Link. "We nearly rode old *Titan* up the street yesterday."

"Up Main Street? You don't say?"

"Bit of excitement for a while."

"I guess there sure was. What happened in the end?"

"We decided to chew up a piece of the jetty instead."

"Not bad! Not bad!"

Mr. Banks straightened up stiffly and eased himself over the side onto the sand.

"Waiting for a final paint job up here, Link," he said, "as soon as you're ready."

"Okay, Dad."

The big man held out his hand. "I'm Brenton P. Huxtable."

Mr. Banks took it. "David Banks," he said simply.

"Glad to know you, Dave. Call me Brent."

"And this is my son, Link."

"My pleasure, Link." His huge hand enveloped Link's and all but crushed it. "My very real pleasure."

He turned back to Link's father, taking a wallet from his pocket. "Now, bill please, Dave."

Link was uncomfortable when the money was being handed over. He was impatient with himself for feeling that way, because it was a perfectly proper business arrangement. Yet somehow he felt guilty. Subtle currents were at work in the town, and strange forces were beginning to polarize. It was something Ripple Bay had never experienced before, something Link couldn't really explain. But he felt like a scab. He felt even worse a little while later when, pressed by Mr. Huxtable, his father went off to the Commercial Hotel to seal the deal with a drink. He watched resentfully as they walked slowly up the ramp together as if they were old mates.

"We're short on drilling mud," he heard the oilman say; "heavy stuff, barite. Got an emergency shipment— two hundred sacks—coming by road from Melbourne. So there's nothing we can do except ferry that stuff right out on the tender and let the cranes haul it up onto the *King*."

His voice began to fade in the distance and Link turned back hurriedly to his painting. He wanted everything to be finished by the time Fire-eater Bukovitch came down looking for his boat.

5

The events that had sent tremors and shocks of change through the age-old peace of Ripple Bay didn't stop with the arrival of the rig and the diesel tender. Early the next morning a new sound pummeled the silence.

Link first heard it in the boat shed. His father had gone to Robe for the day, leaving Link and Tina free to do what they wanted. They had both gone down to the shed to work on an old clapped-out sailing dinghy that Mr. Hackett had promised to give them, provided they could get it seaworthy again.

"What's that?" Link asked.

"What's what?" Tina was using a wood rasp and her ears were full of sawdust and noise.

"Listen."

It was a sound neither of them had ever heard before. Like an eagle slapping the air with wings five meters wide. A chopping, shushing, tearing sound. And right above their heads. They stood quite still, eyes to the roof, listening. Then both guessed the answer simultaneously and yelled it as they ran outside.

"A helicopter!"

It swept over them so low they felt a flurry of wind on their faces. It was a flying skeleton, with a long tail of latticed metal and a fat transparent body, as round as a globule. A skittery, hovering dragonfly of a machine. Link and Tina waved. The machine seemed delighted. It flicked up its tail, put down its head, and came darting steeply toward them—its big blades chomping and thumping urgently, and the little rotor on its tail spinning a circle of light, as it rushed jubilantly down.

Tina's eyes shone. "It's beautiful," she said. "Isn't it a marvelous thing?"

Link laughed. "Hardly beautiful."

"But it's such a happy little fellow. Like a puppy dog in the air."

The exuberant helicopter made two or three more welcoming skitters over them, followed by a wide pass over the bay and the edges of the town, and finally steadied itself above the grassy reserve near the head of the causeway to the jetty.

"Ooh!" Tina exclaimed. "It's getting clucky—like a chook that's going to settle on a nest."

"It's going to land. Come on. Let's get a closer look."

The helicopter began dropping slowly. As it neared the ground it became a man-made willy-willy. The grass was flattened and buffeted; dust was thrown up; bits of paper and litter were hurled about like flashing insects. Then its skids touched the ground and it sat there rocking for a minute. The happy puppy dog had turned into a roaring monster and Tina hung back.

Link turned and waved her on. "It's quite safe," he called, as the big rotor blades hushed slowly to a stop. A moment later a man opened a plastic door on the side of the body bubble and stepped lightly onto the ground.

43

"Good day," he called.

"Hullo."

"Thanks for the wave."

"Thanks for the thanks." They were all slightly awkward at first greetings.

The pilot came walking down toward the boat shed. "I'm supposed to be meeting a guy called Brenton P. Huxtable. From the oil rig. Haven't seen him, I s'pose?"

Link took a few steps forward. "He was here yesterday. Made a spectacular entry."

"Oh? How?"

"Nothing much, really. The tender rammed one of the crayboats at the jetty."

"No! That's a nice start."

"Not much damage. It's all fixed up."

The pilot looked at his watch. "He was going to arrange some shipments from Melbourne—by road I think. I'm supposed to fly him back to the rig."

Tina and Link knew as little as the pilot did. Tina turned to her brother. "Did he stay on shore overnight then?"

"Must have."

The pilot was confident of it. "I'm sure he did."

"Then I know where he is," Link said. "You're not waiting for him, he's waiting for you."

"Where?"

"In the Commercial Hotel."

"Why there?"

"Well there's nowhere else in Ripple Bay where you can spend the night—except maybe in the sand hills."

The pilot laughed, "That's no place for B.P. It's too dry."

He started walking toward the hotel. "You'd think he would have come out, though, at the sound of the chopper. Ornery old tosspot."

It was the beginning of a friendship with the pilot. He was called Bob Joy—a name Tina thought fitted in very well with the happy little helicopter. He started flying regular trips to and from the rig after that, fetching and carrying when the weather was fine—butter, eggs, meat, vegetables, all kinds of fresh food, emergency supplies, directors of the oil company, even sick men from the crew. His helicopter could be seen standing on the reserve at all hours of the day or night—a sight so foreign to the whole spirit of Ripple Bay that visitors used to stop in amazement, as if they'd suddenly come upon something from outer space in the middle of a cow paddock. He also kept Tina and Link up-to-date about events on the rig, and so they were probably the first ones in the town to know when drilling was ready to start.

"Big day tomorrow," Bob Joy said. "We spud in Albatross Two."

Tina was skeptical. "D'you mean it really?"

"That's right."

"When you drill a hole out there, it beats me that the sea doesn't fill it up."

Bob Joy roared with laughter. "You don't know much about drilling oil wells, honey."

"No, I don't."

"Maybe you'll know a lot more before Albatross Two is

finished. She's going to be a deep one—five thousand meters."

Tina was incredulous. "Why, that's miles and miles," she said.

"That's right."

Actually, Tina and Link learned much more quickly than they expected, mainly because of Brenton P. Huxtable and Mr. Hackett. It so happened that occasionally they went to have a meal in the dining room of the Commercial Hotel, especially if Aunt Jessica wasn't well, or wanted a rest from the kitchen, or had gone off to Adelaide to see a doctor or have a holiday. It was a nice old dining room with heavy white tablecloths from long ago, elaborate high-backed chairs, and an enormous carved sideboard that took up half the space along one wall.

On the night before drilling was due to start, Aunt Jessica had been called up to town to see a specialist, so Mr. Banks took Tina and Link to the hotel for what he called a nice, old-fashioned, three-course dinner.

They were surprised at the number of people in the dining room when they arrived—a few tourists who had meandered off the main highway, a salesman caught unexpectedly between motels, a visiting newsman trying to do a story on oil rigs. And, of course, Messrs. Huxtable and Hackett.

"I'll have the chicken soup," Tina said, poring over the menu, "and then roast beef, and . . . and apple pie." Ordering dinner like that gave her a tremendous feeling of warmth and elation which she couldn't really describe— the way her father treated her as the lady in the party and

46

handed her the menu first, the way he and Link waited patiently while she bent over it and made up her mind, the way Liza Potter—Craypot's elder sister—stood respectfully like a good waitress and wrote down her order. It made her feel gracious and important, changed her thin hips and skinny legs into the figure of an actress, and melted her freckles into such peaches-and-cream that Spinner Turner sat panting and drooling at the next table.

She came back from her dream when the soup arrived. At the same moment a loud voice they all recognized very clearly said, "Well if you don't mind me saying so, you have one of the worst sets of blinkers I've met, Doctor Hackett. You sure can't see past your own academic nose." It was Mr. Brenton P. Huxtable at the table behind them, waggling a fork under Mr. Hackett's nose.

Tina was surprised. "Dad, why did he say Doctor Hackett?"

Mr. Banks laughed. "Where he comes from, all college men are 'doctor.' "

"And is Mr. Hackett a college man?" Link asked.

"I guess so. They say he was a professor. He's retired now from whatever he was."

"I suppose that's why he comes down here for his meals so often. He must be awfully lonely living by himself."

They had missed the next part of the discussion, although a vigorous murmur was still coming from the table behind them. Then, quite suddenly, there was another explosion.

"Poppycock! Claptrap!" This time it was so loud that it carried all over the dining room. Conversation stopped.

Tina and Link turned around just in time to see Mr. Huxtable leaning far across the table, prodding his fork into the linen cloth to emphasize his point. "Doctor, I've been in the oil-drilling business for over thirty years and I never heard so much hogwash in all my gasoline-giving life."

He had been drinking in the bar before dinner and seemed to have stayed rather too long. Perhaps mild Mr. Hackett had had an extra glass of claret with his meal too, because even his voice was becoming audible.

"I repeat," he said with great dignity, "there is no need for offshore drilling at all. It's a quite unwarranted risk; and when it's as close to shore as your rig is, then it's an intrusion upon the liberty and rights of others as well."

Mr. Brenton P. Huxtable refilled his glass with a shaking hand to steady himself. Then he took a large mouthful, rolled it about in his red-veined cheeks, and swallowed dramatically.

"Do you know, Doctor Hackett," he said weightily, "that that's exactly where the world's oil is coming from. From offshore wells. The onshore wells are drying up."

"I'm not disputing that," Mr. Hackett said.

His opponent ignored the comment. "Ever since 1950 the writing has been on the wall. 'Get out to sea' has been the message, and out to sea it's been. Look at the rig development since then—fixed platforms, self-elevating platforms, self-propelled rigs, semisubmersible platforms, drill ships, super-high-speed drill ships . . ." There were so many words with "s" sounds in them that Brenton P. Huxtable was beginning to spray his listener with a gentle dew of saliva. Mr. Hackett took out a handkerchief and wiped himself discreetly while the torrent of talk went on.

"Look at the special offshore technology that's been developed," said Mr. Huxtable. "It's a dream, a miracle, and they don't even know about it back on land. It puts science fiction into the kindergarten—men walking about on the seafloor, pipelines like highways under the oceans, wells hundreds of kilometers out to sea feeding crude to the cities, wells spudding in under a thousand meters of water . . ."

He stopped for a hasty gulp of air and wine.

"I still say it isn't necessary." Mr. Hackett's voice spoke very gently. "It isn't worth the cost and the risk."

"Garbage, Doctor! Why, we can barely keep up with the world's needs now. And consumption's rising like a rocket."

"Exactly!"

"So we've got to go offshore."

Mr. Hackett's tone was tense rather than loud. "You know how long it took that oil to form and accumulate?"

Mr. Huxtable laughed deprecatingly. "Well I *am* an oilman, Doctor."

"And you know how much longer it's going to last, Mr. Huxtable? All the oil and gas in this planet? What would you say? Eighty years? That's what the experts think."

"Ah now, Doctor, just how reliable can . . . ?"

"A hundred then. Say a hundred years."

"We-ell . . ."

"And you know when the very first oil well in the world was put down?"

"I sure do—at Titusville, Pennsylvania, in 1859. She was sixty-nine feet deep, and she yielded less than thirty barrels a day." He laughed. "And now we're dragging thirty million barrels a day out of this old world."

"Exactly! So in a total period of two hundred years man

49

will have used up all the oil in the world—oil that it took hundreds of millions of years to create."

Mr. Huxtable waved the argument aside. "If it's there it might as well be used."

"You're a baby with a bankroll," said Mr. Hackett angrily. "You waste it, tear it up, throw it in the air, toss it into the fire. Even stick it up your nappy."

"Hell's teeth, man," cried Mr. Huxtable, jumping up hastily and unsteadily. "Don't you say a thing like that about me."

Mr. Hackett tried to restrain him with his hand. "Sit down! Sit down! It was just a saying. I was talking about mankind as a whole, not about you personally."

"You said I stuck my bankroll up my . . ."

"No I didn't! Look, sit down for heaven's sake. You're disturbing the guests." He caught a glimpse of Tina nearby. "And there are ladies present."

"But you distinctly said I . . ."

"Forget about it! Forget about it! You see what comes of digging oil wells." Mr. Huxtable shook himself free of Mr. Hackett's hand and drew himself up haughtily.

"You don't *dig* oil wells, man! You drill 'em."

"All right! All right! What's the difference?"

Brenton P. Huxtable lowered his arm and looked at Mr. Hackett incredulously. "I don't think you're a doctor at all. I think you're just a little bag of gas. Natural gas."

There was now total silence elsewhere in the dining room. Even the waitresses had stopped serving and stood openmouthed. Brenton P. Huxtable and Mr. Hackett were both standing, leaning across the table toward each other, their voices rising with each sentence.

Ted Stevenson, the hotel manager, came hurrying in from the bar in his shirt sleeves, his fingers still dripping beer froth. He was about to seize the two troublemakers by the elbows and shout his famous cry, "Out! Out you two." But he stopped short when he saw who it was. Then he walked forward politely and indicated the chairs of the two antagonists. "Take a seat, gentlemen."

To everyone's surprise they both sat down, and before either of them could say anything he added quickly, "And I suggest that you keep your discussion as private as possible in the interests of the other diners."

Even the guests were flabbergasted at that. They were used to Ted acting as chucker-out like a brahma bull. But the point told on poor Mr. Hackett. He flushed, looked around the room in furtive embarrassment, and said nothing more for the rest of the meal. Then he got up hastily, bowed unexpectedly to Tina, who was greatly flattered, and made for the door.

Brenton P. Huxtable watched him balefully; he was obviously not prepared to let his antagonist escape without a final blast.

"You and your sort," he yelled, just as Mr. Hackett reached the door. "You're full of that conservation claptrap, but you still drive your cars everywhere." He pointed his finger accusingly and unsteadily. "Yeah, you wouldn't go without your car now, would you, Doctor?"

It was too much. Mr. Hackett drew himself up with cold dignity and turned, his pipe held firmly by its bent stem. "I don't own a car, Mr. Huxtable," he said. The words seemed to remain in the silent room for a long time. Mr. Huxtable put his hand up to his face, as if he'd had a clout

51

on the cheek. For a while nobody seemed to realize that Mr. Hackett had disappeared quickly into the night.

"Well," said Mr. Banks dryly as last, "now we know how things stand."

He shouldn't have spoken. The sound of his voice seemed to rouse Mr. Huxtable into realizing that he was alone and that there was one empty place at the table nearby. "Hi," he said, as if recognizing three long-lost friends. "Mind if I join you?"

"Oh, no," said Tina, self-consciously afraid that her image of ladylike importance was about to be destroyed by the disgrace of a drunken scene.

Mr. Huxtable carried his drink across and flopped down heavily in the vacant chair. He leaned across toward Mr. Banks. "That doctor," he said, obviously still smoldering with the embers of his argument, "he's a shyster. Man, *he is a shyster*. Yes sir."

"Oh," said Mr. Banks noncommittally. "I didn't really hear all that he said."

"Captain, you didn't miss much."

Mr. Huxtable's dim recollection of the boat shed and the slip and old *Titan* had obviously promoted Mr. Banks to the rank of naval officer. "Just a load of claptrap."

"I guess he's genuine in what he thinks," Tina said quietly. She felt she had to defend Mr. Hackett.

"Genuine! Oh sure, they're all genuine. Priests, parsons, committeemen, conservationists, ratbags, and puff adders like that doctor—they're all very genuine." He took another gulp. "Until it comes to giving up the benefits the oil industry has brought 'em."

"He probably thinks there are other alternatives," Link said.

"They wouldn't know, son. They wouldn't know as much as a dicky bird." He snorted grandly. "Most of the things they touch every day come from the petroleum industry. Their whole way of life. Not just natural gas in their ovens and gasoline in their cars, but the roads they drive on. Millions of things from the petrochemical plants. Medicines to keep 'em healthy, and detergents to keep 'em clean, and laxatives to keep 'em purged, and cosmetics to keep 'em beautiful."

His tone was changing, becoming soulful almost, as if mourning man's vast ingratitude. "Every factory in the world," he said suddenly and loudly, "making every single product in the world, would run down in twenty-four hours without the lubricants we give 'em. Every ship and airplane. Half the lights of the world would go out, and the ovens would go cold."

He took another drink and contemplated the injustice of things. "A whole civilization is built on oil. Highways in the sky and roads to the moon. The greatest age in the entire history of the world. On oil. All on oil."

Tina and Link were beginning to feel that he really had a point. They had never stopped to think about oil like that.

"Carpets, pens, paint, plastics, nail polish," Mr. Huxtable was saying, "tar, solvents, Vaseline, carbon black . . ."

"It's a matter of seeing both sides," Mr. Banks broke in, "and of assessing how long the supply will last."

Mr. Huxtable stopped and looked at him closely.

"It's really a job for all mankind," Mr. Banks went on, "because it's our future that's at stake. It needs worldwide planning and control."

Mr. Huxtable decided that he was among friends, even if misguided ones, and let the comment pass.

In the meantime Link was becoming aware of a strange climate in the dining room. People were no longer staring in abashed silence or astonishment, but were speaking in low tones among themselves and looking up at them from time to time. There was something that was almost furtive in the way their eyes were always moving up or down, when Link turned to look.

He began to feel uncomfortable. The same awareness of polarizing forces which he had sensed yesterday swept over him strongly: a feeling that the rig and what it represented was being separated by a clear hard line from Ripple Bay —what it was and what it had always been. That they—he and his family—were being caught and straddled halfway across it. Such a position was never a safe or popular one. And yet here they were in the eyes of the town cementing that impression, hobnobbing with one of the figureheads of the other side. As they had with Bob Joy, the helicopter pilot. As they had accepted their money and work.

"Well I think we'd better be going," Mr. Banks said, "so we'll say good night."

Link tried not to show his haste as he made for the door. But even when he got outside there were shadows on the wind and dark uneasy currents hurrying down toward the harbor.

6

They were on their way to a picnic at the Sea Stacks. Hookie and Tommy Rough were in the lead, followed by Craypot, who was supposed to be the organizer, Spinner Turner and Tina, Martha Lipchynsky and Jana Bukovitch, and a dozen others spread out in a thin straggling line a hundred meters long.

Link came last. He hadn't wanted to go at all, but his father had asked him to keep an eye on Tina and some of the younger ones in case of accidents or emergencies. It was a long way—ten or twelve kilometers at least—and the coastline in most parts was wild and rocky. The Sea Stacks were especially dangerous. They were islands of rock, most of them, standing up in spectacular forms that had been separated from the mainland and shaped by the sea for thousands of years. Huge masses like haystacks some of them were; others were vertical monoliths, pillars and buttresses, arches, humps, and thin columns eroded into points. Some stood in groups, some far out in splendid isolation.

Occasionally the sea had sculpted them into quite strange creatures—here the head of a rhinoceros, there the snout of a crocodile or the bony plates of a dinosaur. Once or twice it had left precarious bridges or causeways, so that man-creatures could walk out onto them and feel the plunge and shock of the sea trembling the world at the very soles of their feet. That was why Mr. Banks had sent Link.

"Keep an eye on them," he had said. "See that they don't do anything stupid."

Link was flattered, in a way, that his father should treat him as an adult—naturally and without fuss. But he was disappointed too, because it would mean missing a trip to Spoonbill Station—a lovely place twenty kilometers inland, where the station homestead looked out over a beautiful big lake that was always swarming with ibises, and spoonbills, and herons. The country out there had boomed when all the swamplands had been drained and turned into rich pasture, and the owners—Mr. and Mrs. Carter—were very wealthy. That was why Mr. Banks couldn't ignore their call. He barely made a living out of the boat shed, with a bit of fishing and part-time work thrown in, and the chance of building a luxury launch for the Carters was like a special present from Father Christmas.

"How long will you be out there, Dad?" Link asked wistfully.

"Don't know. Depends on how much time old Carter wants to spend on drawings and designs."

"Probably be the middle of the afternoon before you get back."

Mr. Banks nodded. "About the same time as you lot, I reckon. It's a long way to the Stacks."

"Especially for some of the little kids." Link's tone had a hint of disgruntlement in it, but his father passed it over. "Watch 'em, Link," he said again. "And take care of yourself."

56

Link regretted his reluctance. "Sure, Dad," he said.

And so here he was, plodding along the rocky cliffs of the old familiar coast, listening to the cries of seabirds. The sea was lashing about ill-naturedly at the foot of the cliffs, and the sound of its restlessness filled his ears. But the wind in his face was cold and bracing, and the day was fine. He found himself glancing constantly and automatically toward the seaward horizon. For there was *Explorer King* as large and implacable as ever. As he moved, so it seemed to move with him. Its presence reached across the intervening wilderness of water, as easily as an intruder crossing a room. If Link looked away, shut his eyes, or blinked, it reared up no less insistently when he looked back. *Explorer King* was permanent.

Meanwhile some of the others had pushed on ahead and formed a little knot at the front of the line, like a tadpole leading its tail. Craypot, Hookie, and Tina were there, and Jana Bukovitch, and Tommy Rough, who was still trying to melt poor Spinner with allure. Tina was wearing a skirt and bodice, much as she hated both. But Aunt Jessica had strong ideas about the need for girls to look feminine and proper, even on picnics, and so she had banned jeans and sloppy pullovers. Luckily Tina had found a disgusting old fishing cap for her head down in the boat shed, and a pair of sawed-off boots for her feet, which had partly restored her reputation among the others. All the same, she still suffered as a result of it. As they came to the last headland near the Stacks and were about to crawl backward down the rocks to the shelf below, a sudden wind gust swept Tina's skirt up over her shoulders and left her bottom sticking roundly out to sea. Craypot whooped from below. "Oo-la-la," he yelled. "I see a secret." Tina nearly lost her footing as she tried to hold down her skirts and simultaneously make a leap for the shelf. She was blushing to the roots of her sandy hair as she picked herself up.

"You looked like an inside-out umbrella coming down," Craypot said, "with a pumpkin in the middle."

The others shouted with laughter, but Tina turned on him in a fury of embarrassment. "You're a smutty-minded dirt-mouth, Craig Potter," she said. "If someone stamped on you, I'll bet you'd squirt squid ink out of your eyeballs."

Craypot was taken aback not only by the anger of her attack but even more by the burning flush of her face. "Ah heck, Tine," he said in a conciliatory tone, "I was only joking."

"Some joke! Just the sort girls love."

Craypot tried to appease her even more. "We'll still barrack for you, Tine—even if your face does look like last week's meat."

Tina could have wept with the humiliation and hurt of it. She could have pummeled the sand with her fists and slapped salt water into her face. But she held herself back. Instead, she lifted her head to the wind and kept it there, turned away from the others, while the hot smart went out of her cheeks and the chafing cold brought moisture to her eyes that hid the tears on the brink of her lids. But for the rest of the picnic she said very little and kept apart. Why, she kept asking herself, did boys have to be so cruel? Why couldn't they recognize the things that hurt? The trip was a disappointment anyway. The tide was too high and

58

the wind too strong for them to go out to the Stacks, and the temperature dropped during the afternoon till it started to numb their cheeks. Worse, some of the younger children had blisters on their feet from the outward trip, and it looked as if they'd have to be helped and jollied all the way home. They sat miserably by the campfire, finishing the last of their hampers. They had exhausted all other topics of talk, and so it was inevitable that they should get around to the one that never wearied.

"They reckon they've got seventy-three men out there," Spinner said, "in the whole crew."

"And no women," Link added.

"And no women," Spinner repeated with a certain relish, looking at Tommy Rough.

She took the bait. "Why not?"

"Well that's obvious," Link said.

"Why is it obvious?"

"Well can you imagine a woman out there?" Spinner said. "She'd only be a blasted nuisance round the place."

"Why would she be?"

"Well she would be, can't you see that? Just because she's a woman. She'd be a . . . a distraction."

Tommy sneered at that. "D'you mean the men couldn't concentrate? They must be pretty weak fish, then."

But Jana interposed seriously. "Nobody should mix with them—not people from the town. My father says we should keep well away; we shouldn't even help them with anything."

Link went to say "Pshaw" so vehemently that he got his tongue caught up in his teeth. Jana thought he was spitting at her. "Link!" she cried, scandalized.

"Sorry! But your father would ban every son, daughter, uncle, aunt, and grandmother he had from even looking at an oil rig if he could. I reckon he hates Dad just for helping to fix his own boat, after the oil tender hit it."

Jana was silent. She liked Link, but she also knew that what he said was true.

"Come on, all up," Link said commandingly. "High time we were heading back." He jostled everyone into action. "Campfire out, hampers packed up, all the rubbish back in the rucksacks." Although Craypot was supposed to be the organizer, it seemed natural to everyone that Link should be giving the orders.

It was a long hard haul. Halfway back little Josie Stevenson petered out altogether with a horribly blistered heel, so Link and Spinner had to take turns carrying her pickaback.

"Whose idea was this picnic?" Spinner said, panting and staggering under Josie. "We've got some brilliant characters in our town." Everyone else started to pick on Craypot too, and to tease him for all that had gone wrong. Perhaps the hurt of their ridicule sharpened his sensitiveness to others; perhaps he was already aware of his own accord. But when they were within a few kilometers of home, he caught up with Tina deliberately and walked beside her for a minute.

"Tina," he said. "About . . . about what I said." She looked at him stonily but said nothing, and so Craypot had to blunder on. "Well . . . I'm . . . I'm sorry if I hurt you. I . . . I didn't mean to, honest."

She could have kissed him. She could have run off the

headland high into the air and flown around in an arc like a racing petrel. She could have held her head back in the wind and cried for gratitude.

"Thanks, Craypot," she said. "I'm glad." She turned and faced him and, seeing his anxious look, suddenly beamed a huge genuine smile. "Really I am."

"Good," he said. "I'm glad, too."

They were nearing home at last. The big sand hill was in sight, and bits of the country beyond, but the town and the bay were still hidden. It was much later than they had expected and the evening was already closing in. As they came around a hump in the coast near the headland of their own bay, Tina stopped short. "Look," she said. "Who's that?" The others stopped too, jostling and peering.

"Strangers," Spinner said. "Ever seen 'em before, Link?"

"No."

There were six or seven of them, children and teenagers, crawling about on the cliffs and the rocky beach half a kilometer away. As Link's party watched, they saw the other group gather together in a knot near one spot where some-one seemed to have found something exciting. Tina sud-denly gave a cry, half fear, half anger. "Oh no!"

The others turned to look at her, astonished. "What's up?"

But she was already ahead of them, running at full speed. She half turned once, waving them on impatiently with her arm. "Come on!" she yelled. "Come on, hurry! They've found Piglet."

When Link and his companions reached the spot, Tina had already joined battle with the intruders. She had been right about them. Three of the bigger boys had sticks, which they had been using to prod the fairy penguins out of their burrows. They had several of them, held cruelly and carelessly by their legs or flippers. But worst of all, one of them had Piglet. And Tina was going for him like a light tank, with guns blazing.

"Put him down!" she shouted. "Put him down this minute."

The boy had hair the color of pale straw and a white face, pocked with pimples. He was belligerent. "Why should I?"

Tina blew up. None of the others had ever seen her like this before. She raised a piece of driftwood she had found on the way back and held it in both hands like a club. "Put him down this instant or, so help me, I'll clobber you senseless."

Strawhead took a step back but refused to release Piglet. "Why should I put it down? Penguins like this are as much for me as for you or anyone else."

Tina's eyes were twin blowtorches. "Penguins are for penguins, not for creeps like you, or any other people either. So put him DOWN!" She had finished with words and moved in to the attack, her club raised.

Strawhead retreated, but collided with two or three of his confederates behind him. They were all being squeezed on the narrowing shelf of rock that ran in front of Piglet's burrow. Tactically they were being cornered by the far larger numbers in Link's party. Strawhead capitulated.

"Oh, all right," he said vindictively. "Take the smelly thing." He half released, half threw, Piglet onto the shelf.

62

For a second or two the little penguin waddled about confused, but then Tina dropped to her knees and called, "Piglet, here Piglet," and made a sucking noise with her tongue.

Piglet turned, recognized her among the medley of legs and faces, and ran toward her. Tina had tears in her eyes as she held him in her arms. "Oh, Piglet!" She stood up, holding the little penguin against her shoulder like a baby. He nibbled at her ear.

"Did you see that, Link?" she asked, turning to her brother. "That's what he used to do at home, when he was pleased with something or feeling affectionate." She rubbed the nape of his neck and clicked her tongue. "You haven't forgotten us, have you, Piglet? No you haven't."

During all this, Strawhead and his colleagues were standing uncomfortably at the narrow end of the rock shelf. But now they made a move to escape. "If you let us get past," Strawhead said, "we'll take ourselves out of here."

Tina stood facing them, barring the way. Her anger had barely cooled at all. "Now you lot," she said, "crawl into those hollows, and we're all going to take a turn prodding you with sticks. Go on, in you go!"

They were flabbergasted. She spoke so coldly and vehemently that for a moment they thought she was serious.

Strawhead spoke ingratiatingly. "You're having us on."

"No!" said Tina, opening her eyes as wide as an owl's. "But by all the ghosts of Ripple Bay, if we catch you interfering with the penguins again, we'll have you on all right —with clubs and prodding sticks. We'll give you plum-colored eyeballs and cauliflower ears, so help me."

Strawhead was completely deflated. "Well, we didn't know. We only arrived today."

"Sure," said Tina contemptuously, "and you'll be gone tomorrow. But you'll do as much damage as you can while you're here. You're like all the other tourists—if you're not disturbing the fairy penguins here, you're frightening off the pelicans on Pelican Island, or the swans on the Coorong, or the seals on Kangaroo Island. Till there'll be no wildlife left in South Australia at all and we'll be forced to go and look at *people* in cages instead."

Link was smiling. He couldn't help it. The whole thing looked so incongruous—the intruders lined up like naughty boys, Tina as vocal as an angry mum—with a surprised-looking penguin peering over her shoulder like a baby about to be burped, and all the rest of them getting an impromptu lecture on conservation.

"Gosh, I didn't know it was a pet penguin," Strawhead flustered.

"He's not a *pet*!" Tina thundered. "He's *free*. Can't you get that into your head?"

"Well, it's so . . . so sort of friendly."

"We helped him once when he was so sick that he would have died. And so he loves us, just as we love him. But he lives his own life—out here. And we're going to see that it stays that way—without interference." She put so much emphasis on the last two words that everyone thought she was going off into orbit again. But Strawhead prevented it.

"All right! All right! We've got the message."

"You'd better have the message."

Link thought it was time to intervene. "Come on, Sis,"

he said in a big-brotherly kind of way, "time to get off home. It'll be dark soon."

Tina conceded the point reluctantly and finally moved aside to let the intruders get by. Strawhead shuffled past, keeping as far from her as he could.

"Beats me how you can tell him apart from all the rest of 'em," he said.

"I could tell him in a colony of a thousand," she said proudly, "like a mother bird with her own baby."

Spinner and one or two of the small fry whistled at that. "Listen to Tina," they said. "She's getting clucky herself."

Tina ignored them. She wasn't even embarrassed, although she did notice with a pulse of gratitude that Craypot hadn't joined in. "In any case," she said with a superior air, "he's got his own little tag—fixed to his leg by a Commonwealth research scientist."

Even Strawhead was interested in that—especially since he'd escaped successfully and was now standing well clear of her. "Oh? What does it say?"

"It says *Piglet, Ripple Bay, South Australia!* And the date."

"At least he won't get lost."

"He certainly won't." Tina looked back at the group as they departed up the headland. "And he won't get prodded out of his burrow anymore either."

Strawhead didn't reply, but the private comment of one of his gang came back clearly to all of them: "Strike me dead, Mike, she doesn't let up much does she? She's worse than old Auntie Maude."

Link roared. "Did you hear that, Sis?"

"Yes I did! And I don't care. With that sort you have to clobber it into their skulls with a boat hook."

Even Craypot laughed. "You sure did that, Tine. I don't think they'll pull Piglet out again."

But Tina was far from easy. "They might do it just for spite."

"Not them," Craypot said. "I recognize them now. They're relatives of the folk who own the house next door."

"That lot," Spinner said. "Then at least they'll be gone in a week or two."

"Yes, and then they'll send another bunch of no-hopers down," Craypot said, "and so on, and on, and on. Enough to drive you mad. We have to live next to 'em—Mum, and me and Liza, and poor old Mr. Hackett."

"Must drive him mad."

"You ought to hear him. He reckons he's going to leave Ripple Bay soon; going to try to find a quiet spot in the middle of the Simpson Desert."

They straggled on home through the last gloom of twilight, Tina having given Piglet a ceremonious farewell.

"He won't even find peace out there before long," Tommy Rough said. "There'll be people everywhere."

Link looked out to sea. The red beacon lights of *Explorer King* had come on, winking a warning to all navigation. As he watched, the bright floodlights came on too. He tried to imagine the scene out there on the rig—men toiling with tin hats on, big diesels roaring, metal clanking on metal, and far below them, below even the seafloor itself, the drill-bit grinding relentlessly through the rock.

On and on, deeper and deeper. Twenty-four hours a day, seven days a week. Ceaselessly, inflexibly, relentlessly.

"You're right, you know," he said, speaking partly to Tommy and partly to himself. "There'll be people everywhere. And pity poor old Earth."

7

The walk to the Sea Stacks had exhausted Link and Tina more than they knew, and they both slept unexpectedly late the next morning. When Link woke up, the sun was high above Ripple Bay, and sunlight as yellow as quince skins was lying on the slats of the venetian blinds beside his bed.

"Cripes," he said to himself, turning to look at the clock on his bedside dresser. "What time is it?" He squinted this way and that to get the hands in the right perspective. "Jeepers! Nine o'clock!"

He listened carefully for signs from outside. Not a sound. "Place is deserted," he thought. "Where is everybody?" His room was part of an enclosed verandah running along the side of the house. He heaved himself out of bed, tiptoed into the passage, and peered stealthily into Tina's room. He smiled. The blankets were sticking up in a solitary hill in the middle of the bed, and a mane of sandy-colored hair lay tousled over the pillow. She was fast asleep in her special early-morning position—lying on her stomach with her bottom stuck up in the air.

Link went on quietly to the kitchen. Nobody there. Breakfast was over; washing up had been done. He peeped into his father's bedroom and finally even into Aunt Jessica's. Beds were all made, blinds up, everything terribly ordered and shipshape.

He stood for a while at the front door looking at the

town. Aunt Jess must have gone down to get some things —bread from Archie Armstrong at the bakery, meat from Ridge's Ripple Bay Quality Meat Store, and maybe groceries from Otto Holstein. Link smiled as he pictured poor old Otto trying to thaw out Aunt Jessica so early in the morning. He wouldn't have a hope.

The smile was still on Link's face as he lifted his gaze to the blue bay and the open sea beyond it. It stayed there for a moment and then slowly changed into a ridiculous expression of amused amazement.

For going out through the heads was old *Titan*, and behind her at the end of a thick towline was Brenton P. Huxtable's tender, loaded to the gunwales with sacks of barite and barrels of drilling mud for shipment out to *Explorer King*.

"Cods and catfish!" Link exclaimed. "Hey," he yelled as he recovered, "come and look at this." His voice rattled about inside the empty house so loudly it finally woke Tina. She came padding up the passage, rubbing her ribs with one hand and her eyes with the other.

"What's up?"

"Get a load of this." Link pointed across the bay.

"What is it?" Tina asked.

"Wake up, Bright Eyes! The boats! Look at the boats."

She found the range at last. "Gosh, it's *Titan*; towing someone."

"Towing *someone*!" Link exclaimed. "Towing Mr. Bigwig Huxtable's tender, with the mighty out-of-this-world engines, that's what." He laughed. "How's that for a comedown?"

"Has it broken down, then?"

"Must have."

"How could he get old *Titan* to help, though?"

"Hired her, I guess—from Dad. Must have swallowed gall to do a thing like that."

"D'you think *Titan* can do it?"

Link scoffed. "She used to haul fifty-thousand-tonners. She'd pull that thing with her little toe. She's just flexing her muscles."

"He must have got onto Dad early this morning."

"Yes, while you were still asleep."

Tina looked scornfully at Link's crumpled pajamas. "You dressed for tennis?"

"No, golf actually. New style. Like it?"

Tina gazed back at old *Titan*. "I suppose Dad'll be out all day, towing that thing."

"He won't be back till after lunch, that's for sure. Depends on how long they take to unload."

"Is there more of that guk to be taken out after this?"

"Two more loads, I'd say. More stuff came in last night by road from Adelaide."

Tina shut the front door and started to walk back to her room. Halfway down the passage she stopped and looked back at Link. "Where's Aunt Jess? She hasn't gone out on that thing too, has she?"

Link shouted with laughter. "Jesse James? She'd rather ride a brumby."

"Where is she then?"

"Shopping, I guess."

Tina suddenly remembered something. "Have you bought her a birthday present yet?"

"Not yet. I haven't had time."

"Well you'll have to make time. It's her birthday tomorrow."

"Have *you* bought anything?"

"I'm getting it today."

"Get something for me, will you?"

Tina was sharp. "You do your own shopping. And don't forget! She hasn't got many friends or relatives."

"I guess not."

"It'd be awful if nobody remembered your birthday."

"I'd feel lonely, I guess."

"Lonely! You'd feel unwanted. That would be worse. So get her a present."

"Sure, I won't forget."

Link strode back to his room. "Time we got dressed. I'm off to the slip to find out what's going on."

When he arrived at the beach he found the fishermen as sour as lemons. In order to load the cargo that morning the crew of the tender had virtually taken over the jetty. A big mixing bin had been set up onshore, and the drilling mud had been pumped into special pods built belowdecks in the tender. Hydraulic lines still lay about on the jetty like huge pythons, their open ends oozing slowly. And then, to make matters worse, the crew had loaded hundreds of bags of barite and barrels of specially treated cement, trundling the heavy loads on trolleys to the deepwater berth and then swinging them aboard with their own winches. But twice a barrel had gone overboard—one smashing a new bollard, the other landing foursquare on the hatch of Bert Thompson's crayboat lying alongside and staving it in so completely that it looked like a dog's kennel that had been sat on by an elephant.

"They pay!" Mario Bukovitch growled darkly. "Santa Maria, they pay all right."

John Leckie was less furious, but just as determined. "It's getting so bad that a man can't even use his own moorings anymore. We might as well beach our boats and hand the bay over to the oil company."

"And what they want with mud?" Mario asked in disgust. "Who I like to know wanta take mud to the sea bottom? Is plenty there already. Only madmens and lunatics, don't you think?"

Even John Leckie was bamboozled. "Beats me. I always thought the idea was to get mud out when you're digging a hole, not put it back in."

"That's right! They dig the hole, then fill her up." Mario rolled his eyes to heaven.

Link stood on the jetty shading his eyes against the sun. "Old *Titan* is coming back," he said after a while, "but she's alone. She's left the tender out at the rig."

"Best thing," Mario rumbled. "And I hope she sink." He paused. "Your father," he went on after a while, "he shouldn't help them. Is no good."

Link flushed and was about to speak out in defense of his father, but John Leckie intervened. "They're probably having a look at the tender—finding out what's wrong."

They all stood watching as *Titan* flopped and plunged back toward the bay, her bow alternately up in the air like a beacon and then down out of sight. Now and again, when she charged through a big wave, she was hung with white lace. As they watched, something rose up suddenly behind

her from the rig. Link pointed excitedly. "Look, the helicopter." They saw it rise as always, like a busy dragonfly;
then it flicked up its tail, put down its head, and banked
sharply.

John Leckie was puzzled. "Which way is he heading?"

"Not this way," Mario said.

"Southeast by the look of it. Making for Mount Gambier." Link puckered his brows.

"Must be urgent. He only goes down there when it's an
emergency, or when he's ferrying passengers."

They watched the helicopter skitter away in the distance,
the sun glinting on the round globe of its body.

"I guess we'll find out," Link said as it faded from
sight.

"Sure." John Leckie took out a packet of cigarettes.
"Your father'll probably know, anyhow."

Link's father did know. He barely waited for *Titan* to
stop her wheezing and coughing at the wharf before he
called out loudly. "Hey, Link! Over here."

Link swung himself down onto the deck. "What happened to the tender?"

"Just ignition trouble. They're fixing it out at the rig."
Mr. Banks had that queer expression which goes with people who are brimming with news. "How would you like to
be an oilman?" he said. "For a couple of weeks?"

Link looked at him incredulously. "I'm not with you,
Dad."

"Out there. On the rig."

"What?"

"That's right."

"Me? Out there?"

"Yes, you."

"When?"

"Now."

"Why?"

"Cook's offsider broke his arm. Young lad. Be out for a couple of weeks."

"So that's what was up. The helicopter, I mean."

"Yes. Flying him to hospital. In Mount Gambier."

"We saw."

Mr. Banks looked at Link quizzically. "Fantastic wages, son. You'll make money."

"Why me, though?"

"They need someone in a hurry—by this afternoon. Mr. Huxtable thought of you. He put in a word."

"Jeepers."

"He reckons you could do the job with your hands tied. So do I."

Link was flabbergasted. Uncertainty, excitement, uneasiness, happiness raced through his feelings all at once. He looked at his father. "What d'you think, Dad? Should I take it?"

"If you want to. Your decision, Link."

"I wouldn't miss any school, would I?"

"Not if it's only for two weeks. School doesn't start again for another three."

"Well I reckon I will."

His father climbed up onto the jetty. "Then you'd better come home and get packed. Bob Joy is calling in on his way back from the hospital. He'll be here in an hour. If you're going, he'll expect you to be ready."

74

"Mackerel! One hour."

Link leaped after his father and ran on ahead. "Tell Aunt Jess if you see her," he called back. "She must be down the street, shopping."

As he ran up the causeway at the head of the jetty he almost collided with Craypot and Hookie, who had just come in from a short fishing trip on *Albacore*.

"Watch out," Link said. "Look where you're going."

Craypot snorted. "All right, Cannonball. What's your big hurry?"

Link checked himself. Quite suddenly, for some reason, he didn't want them to know. He ducked the question by asking a different one. "Good trip? Plenty of fish?"

"Scarce as snakes' legs," Hookie said. "I reckon that great oil heap out there is frightening them off."

Craypot dived his hand into a bucket he was carrying. "But we got something for you, Link. Here."

He held up an octopus by one of its tentacles and thrust it at Link. "For your lunch." The octopus scrabbled about madly with its seven other tentacles, and two of them managed to grip one of Link's legs. It was perhaps half a meter across—and it gripped like rawhide. Link yelled and jumped back, threshing about with his hands and kicking wildly. Fortunately his jeans were coarse, and Craypot still held on to one tentacle; and so with a violent jerk from Link and a heave from Craypot, the thing came free and was dropped back with difficulty into the bucket.

Link was still flapping about. "Ooh, I hate those things," he said. "They give me the creeps."

"Beauty, ain't he?" Hookie boasted.

"Oh, sure. I'll put him in your bed if you like, so you can cuddle him tonight."

Craypot laughed hugely. "Might be a girl octopus." He turned to Hookie. "You'd know when she had you in her arms, Hook." And he whooped about with his knees bent and his face screwed up at his own joke.

Link pushed past them. "Sorry, fellows, I've got to go." And before they could say anything else he was gone.

Even then he wasn't free of interruptions. Halfway up the street he heard a high piping voice yelling, "Link! Link!" and a second later Tina came rocketing out of Holstein's store with a big parcel clutched in both hands. She ran up to him, panting, her eyes bright with news. "Link, have you got two dollars?"

It was an opening that always made him cautious. "What for?"

"Never mind what for. Have you?"

"I could have."

"A two-dollar note?"

"Maybe."

"Give it to me." She held out her hand.

"Not till you tell me what for."

Tina was impatient. "For Jesse James's present, Ningnong." She put the parcel down in the middle of the street and started to open up the brown wrapping paper at the top. "See," she said eagerly, folding the paper back. "Isn't it terrific?"

Link peered forward woodenly. "What is it?"

"Oh, for heaven's sake!" Tina opened the parcel even further. "Look!"

"Is it a basket—with a lid?"

Tina was beside herself. "Of course it's a basket, Brainstorm. A sewing basket. She's always wanted one."

"Who? Six-Gun?"

Tina gave up. "Oh no! Dad's been hankering after embroidery threads for years."

Link began to get angry. "Well I didn't know what the devil you were on about—rushing out into the street like a maniac, yak-yak-yakking a lot of garbage in bits and pieces."

Tina knew her brother well and pulled back. "Sorry. But it was the only present that suited Aunt Jess. Apart from that there wasn't a thing. And Mr. Holstein was very nice —he reduced it a lot. I paid him half the money and he let me have it. I said I'd be back with the rest in a minute." She held out her hand again. "So give me two dollars."

Link was still nettled, but he started to fish for the money in his pocket. "Too bad if I haven't got it," he said grumpily.

"You have," she answered cheekily. "I saw it on your dresser yesterday."

"Women!" he said in an old-young tone, exactly like his father's. But he handed her the money all the same.

"It'll be from both of us—the present," she said. "Aunt Jess'll like that."

"She'd better; that's all the money I've got."

"Your good deed," Tina said, skipping off irritatingly back to the shop. "Mind the present for a sec, will you?"

"Look, Sis, I'm in an awful hu—" Link started to say,

but he bit the sentence short and was glad she hadn't heard. Again he had that strange, half-guilty feeling, as if he was on the verge of doing something that was wrong.

"What a galah," he thought to himself as he watched the empty doorway through which she'd disappeared. "Left standing in the middle of the street with a half-unwrapped sewing basket. A fellow must be off his crumpet."

"Hullo, hullo," said a flat harsh voice behind him. "If it isn't Ali Baba with a basket of treasure, right here in the middle of Ripple Bay."

Link groaned. "Oh, no!"

It was Craypot and Hookie again, sauntering up with supercilious looks on their faces. Craypot still carried the bucket and Hookie had an armful of tackle. They peered elaborately at Tina's parcel.

"New kind of craypot, is it?" Hookie said. "With varnished wickerwork—and a lid." They both bent to examine the lid. "With hinges," Hookie added.

"It's a special kind of pot," Craypot said. "Instead of the crayfish being on the outside trying to get in, you put him on the inside so he's trying to get out."

"Ah knock it off," Link said wearily. "You're both as wet as seaweed—and just about as sparkling." He searched the shop with his gaze, trying to will Tina into hurrying back. He should really have known the other two better than to take his eyes off them, because as he was looking about desperately for a sign of his sister, Craypot whipped out the octopus from the bucket and, while Hookie held open the lid, dropped it cleanly and silently into the basket. It was a fat-bodied basket, rather like an old-fashioned cooking pot,

78

and the lid fitted snugly. The octopus appeared to accept its new home, for it settled quietly on the bottom.

"We'll leave you to it then, Ali," Craypot said. "Let us know if you find any more treasure."

"Or thieves," Hookie added.

"Why don't you go and catch fleas," Link called. "You ought to be in a monkey cage."

Luckily Tina returned just then and he was able to get away at last. "They should call you Flash for short," he said sarcastically. "Come on."

She grabbed her parcel and followed him, pushing the brown paper wrapping back into place. "What's the tearing hurry? You got ants in your pants or something?" Link was already striding on ahead.

"I'll tell you when we get home," he said.

When they walked into the kitchen their father and Aunt Jessica were already there. They both turned. "I've just been telling your aunt the news, Link," Mr. Banks said.

"Yes, and I can't say I'm any too pleased." Aunt Jessica was never one for niceties; her tone suggested vinegar mixed with hydrochloric acid. "I'm surprised at your father permitting it, I must say."

Mr. Banks was unruffled. "It's his decision, Jessica," he said quietly. "He's old enough to decide for himself."

"I doubt that," she replied curtly. "Out there with that riffraff—quite apart from the danger."

Tina's eyes were like organ stops. She looked in bewilderment from one to the other, her mouth half open on the verge of a question, but every time she tried to speak she was cut off before she could start.

"It'll be an adventure for him, Jessica," Link's father answered. "And a wonderful education. An experience in a lifetime."

"That's what I'm afraid of," she replied coldly.

At last Tina found a chink to push her question into. "Will someone please tell me what's going on?" she called out in a tense, high-pitched voice. "What's happening to Link? What on earth is he going to do?"

Mr. Banks waited for his son to speak, but Link said nothing. "He's been offered a job on the oil rig," he said at last, "for a couple of weeks."

Tina's organ-stop eyes popped out a further notch. "He *has*?"

"Yes."

"On *Explorer King*? Link? An oilman?"

"A kitchen roustabout," Aunt Jessica said scornfully. "A pot walloper, a slushy."

Tina's face fell. She liked romantic heroes. "You don't have to take it, do you?"

For the first time since they'd walked inside, Link spoke. "No, but I'm going to."

"More fool you." There were icicles in Aunt Jessica's tone. Tina was still confused. "Are they going to pay you?"

Mr. Banks laughed out loud. "Are they! He'll get more in two weeks than I make in a month."

"I'll believe that when I see it." Aunt Jessica wasn't in the mood to concede anything at all. "And even if he does, it shows how far they've got to go just to get somebody to work out there with those . . . those heathens."

80

Mr. Banks scoffed. "It'll be an adventure," he repeated. "Like the cabin boys in the old stories."

Tina's imagination recovered from Aunt Jessica's picture of pot scouring and potato peeling. "Like Jim Hawkins in *Treasure Island* finding the pirate's treasure."

"Working with pirates," Aunt Jessica said. "At least that part is true."

Mr. Banks ignored her. "If *Explorer King* strikes oil," he said, "really strikes oil, there'll be treasure all right, more than Robert Louis Stevenson ever dreamed of. It'll make the pirates' hoard look like weekend pocket money."

Link looked at the clock. "Gosh, I'd better pack. Bob Joy'll be here in a minute to pick me up."

The announcement seemed to startle everybody, even Aunt Jessica. "I'll make up a snack," she said, "and a cup of coffee. It'll probably be the last decent thing you'll get for the next two weeks."

Link and Tina looked at each other and winked. They knew that Aunt Jessica's bark was always a lot worse than her bite; she was really very generous at heart. As likely as not she'd turn around now and mother Link till he was half suffocated.

"Pack all your warm jumpers," she said, busying herself with cake and biscuits. "And thick underclothes, and socks, and scarves, and your greatcoat. It'll be terribly cold out there."

"Yes, Aunt Jess," Link answered obediently.

"And warm pajamas."

"Yes, Aunt Jess."

"And a balaclava."

"Yes, Aunt Jess."

"And don't forget . . ."

"Your *toothbrush!*" Tina and Mr. Banks yelled it together. They all laughed, even Aunt Jessica. It seemed a good note to escape on, so Link ran out to his room and started stuffing his things into an old suitcase. A few minutes later Tina came out surreptitiously with a serious question.

"Link?"

"Yes, Sis."

"If you're leaving in a minute I think we ought to give Jesse James her present now."

"Her birthday present?"

"Yes."

"Be better to wait till the morning, wouldn't it?"

"Not if you're going to be away."

"I think she'd like something on her real birthday."

"Dad'll give her something nice. And I'll give her breakfast in bed and fuss about a bit."

Link was throwing socks and undershirts into his case. "Well, if you like."

"I'm sure she'd prefer it—for you to be there when your present is opened."

"Half my present."

Tina laughed. "All right, she can open your half and leave mine till the morning."

"Better hurry up then," Link said. "Bob Joy won't be long."

Tina ran for the door. "I'll quickly write out the card and get some colored wrapping paper. I saved up a piece from Dad's birthday."

Five minutes later they were all back in the kitchen again. Aunt Jessica had a regular spread arranged on the table, and a big tin of biscuits ready for Link to take with him. "You don't know what things are going to be like out on that oil rig," she said. "They'll only feed you once a day, I'll be bound."

"Like the seals," Link said, grinning.

Mr. Banks guffawed. "Meals around the clock, twenty-four hours a day," he said. "Good food, good living quarters, air-conditioned comfort. A lot better than home from home."

And then, before Aunt Jessica could make a rejoinder, Tina came tiptoeing in with her big, colored parcel. "For your birthday," she said a little breathlessly, "because Link can't be here tomorrow morning. Many happy returns." And she kissed her aunt roundly on the cheek.

Aunt Jessica melted like butter in the sun. "You dear kids," she said. "Bless you both."

For a terrible moment Link thought she was going to flop about all over him. But Tina handed her the card just then, so there had to be a good deal of envelope opening and card extracting, and then a minute's silence for reading Tina's inscription: "To our dear Aunt-Mother, and the best cook in the world. Happy Birthday, with lots of love from Tina and Link." Again there was a momentary danger of arms around necks and dewy kisses, but it passed in a gush of thanks and a flush of excitement on Aunt Jessica's cheeks while she tackled the wrapping on the parcel.

"What is it, I wonder," she said, shaking it. She went on removing the colored paper. "Do you know, David?" she asked, looking up at her brother-in-law.

Mr. Banks was standing like a patriarch by the stove. "I wouldn't have a clue. Not a clue."

"I'll bet you do know," she said. Then the outer paper was off at last, and she sat prodding the brown paper. "Goodness, more wrapping. I can't *imagine* what's in it." She gave the impression of a woman who had never received many presents in her life, someone who was experiencing what she should have experienced as a little girl. "Gosh, I'd better hurry," she said suddenly, "or I'll be making Lincoln late." With a stern pull she stripped off the brown paper at a swoop, and there at last the gift stood revealed on the table.

"A sewing basket! Oh how lovely."

The others shifted from one foot to the other and smiled with her in her joy.

"Really, it's just what I've always wanted. It really is."

"I'm glad you like it," Tina said. "I hoped you would."

"Yes," said Link, a little lamely. "So did I."

"You dear kids!" Aunt Jessica was so genuinely moved that Link moved back a step in case she should now be overcome by a violent urge for kissing. But she was a hard-bitten, practical woman too, so she stood up in a business-like way to get on with the meal. Her hands were still on the basket. "I really do appreciate it," she said in a final sort of way. "Thank you both very much."

She unfastened the lid and examined the weave, testing it between her fingers for fiber and texture.

"Neatly woven," said Mr. Banks. "Where was it made?"

"In the East, I guess," Link said. "Do you know, Sis?"

Without any of them being aware of it, a tentacle pushed

84

its way through the slit of the partly open basket and wavered tentatively from side to side, like a hand feeling about blindly on top of a shelf.

"No," Tina answered. "Singapore or Hong Kong, I guess."

A second tentacle joined the first, and then a third, all of them prospecting the air vigorously like Medusa's snakes, fastening and unfastening their grips energetically on the wickerwork sides. It was obvious that whatever kind of body they were joined to was following them up steadily toward the open air.

"We import a lot of things like this from Taiwan these days," Mr. Banks said.

A fourth tentacle came up and methodically probed the circumference of the basket. Aunt Jessica had one hand resting on the edge. The tentacle came up to it, hesitated for a second, and started twining about the sleeve of her blouse at the wrist. For a moment it didn't register with her. By now the body of the octopus had reached the lip of the basket and the remaining tentacles were busy scrabbling about for something else to hold on to. The one at Aunt Jessica's blouse had completed one full circle of her wrist and was twining up her arm as rapidly as a tendril from Jack's magic beanstalk.

At last she felt it, and looked down.

"*E-e-e-e-e-k!*"

The first shriek was so intense that Mr. Banks clutched his chest, as if the stab of a coronary attack had pierced it. Link had never heard anything like it. It jolted him in a great wave of shock and fear that left his face a sickly white.

Then Tina saw the squirming mass hanging on to her Aunt's arm and joined the shrieking. High-pitched and ear-shattering, their squeals echoed and rebounded about the kitchen. It was oral terror; horror turned into sound.

Aunt Jessica had recoiled from the table, dragging the creature with her, still fastened firmly to her arm. For a second the basket hung grotesquely, joined to its owner by the writhing thongs between. Then it dropped off and bounded away into the doorway. Shrieking and sobbing, Aunt Jessica lunged about near the sink, her body convulsing, her arms threshing wildly and the octopus flailing up and down like a cat-o'-nine-tails. Tina stood by the table, rigid and aghast, her hands up to the sides of her head, her mouth open, the shrieks pouring out endlessly. Link also seemed too paralyzed to move.

Only Mr. Banks recovered quickly. He sprang forward, seized Aunt Jessica by the arm and, holding it firmly in both hands like the handle of an axe, brought it down hard and sharp near the edge of the sink. The body of the octopus crashed down on the stainless steel. Mr. Banks repeated the movement. And then again, and again, and again. He was grunting through his breath. "Let go, you devil! Let go! Let go!" Pummeled and stunned, the octopus began to relax its grip at last, and all but the end of the last tentacle came free. Link, recovering himself, leaped forward and pinned its body in the sink with a rolling pin, while Mr. Banks seized a filleting knife and plunged it into the jellylike head. Then he ripped the hold of the last suckers from the blouse, grabbed the dying creature by the tip of a tentacle and, running to the kitchen door, hurled it outside into the garden.

86

Aunt Jessica was lolling against the sink now, sobbing uncontrollably. Her face was sickly and clammy, with a hint of blue in its pallor, and her breath wheezed from her heaving chest. Tina ran to her.

"Here, sit down, Aunt Jess."

But Mr. Banks intervened. "No, into the bedroom. Tina, run and pull back the bedspread; Link, help me with your aunt." And so they got Aunt Jessica down the passage, still sobbing and shuddering periodically from a kind of uncontrollable revulsion, and lifted her onto her bed at last. Mr. Banks pulled the blinds. "Now, you stay there, Jess," he said kindly but firmly. "I'll ring Doc Harper and get him to give you a shot." He shepherded Tina and Link out of the room and partly closed the door.

As soon as they were back in the kitchen he turned on Tina and Link. He was white with anger. He looked at them contemptuously for a second and then let them have it. "What a stupid thing to do," he thundered. "What a lamebrained, idiotic, empty-headed, lunatic thing to do! You know how your aunt feels about things like that; about any crawling things—even centipedes and spiders. They revolt her, make her flesh creep. Yet you bring in a thing like that—an octopus. Of all things, *an octopus.*"

Link and Tina both opened their mouths to start a story of explanation and apology, but they did not get a chance.

"You could have killed her, doing a thing like that. With her asthma. As it is, it'll bring on an attack as sure as God made apples. So perhaps you'll think about that when you enjoy your little joke."

"Dad," Link said, coming forward earnestly, "we—"

"And in her *birthday* present," his father went on furiously. "Of all things, in her birthday present! What a callous, coldhearted thing to do! And to a woman who's been a mother to you. I ought to put you both over my knee and leather the hides off you."

Tina was close to tears and couldn't stand it any longer. "Dad," she blurted out. "We didn't do it. We didn't even know about it."

But instead of helping matters, this only made her father more furious. "Don't give me that!" he yelled. "What do you take me for—a chump?"

"We really didn't!"

"Look, my girl," he said in a cold, hard voice. "I'll leather you yet. If you try to get out of this by lying, that's exactly where you'll end up."

"It's true! We didn't know about it!"

Her father marched toward her so decisively that she blanched. He waggled his finger under her nose. "Do you expect me to believe that you can bring a big parcel in here, all wrapped up in colored paper and all, and not know that thing's inside it?"

Tears were dripping from Tina's lower eyelids now, but she stuck to her guns. "I know it sounds queer, but it's true for all that."

"It's not true!" her father shouted back. "That thing couldn't have been out of the water more than a quarter of an hour. It was still fresh and lively. And that's why you two insisted on giving the parcel to Aunt Jess today. So the thing would still be crawling about; so it would frighten the life out of her."

Tina was appalled at the imputation. "No! No!" Her sobs overwhelmed her now. "We gave . . . gave it to Aunt

88

Jess . . . today . . . because . . . because Link is going away
. . . away, like we said. We didn't know . . . about the oc . . .
the toc . . . about the tocoptupus."

Link came forward. "You've got to believe her, Dad.
She's as scared of things like that as Aunt Jess is. She could
never put it in there, never pick it up even."

His father seemed half inclined to accept the point, but
turned on him instead.

"So you're the mastermind!" he said. "Maybe it's just as
well you're going out on that rig. The longer you stay away
from your aunt the better."

A chopping sound swept over the house just as he said it,
and they all paused to listen.

"There's the helicopter now," Mr. Banks said. "Better
pack up and go." He went over to the phone. "I must ring
Doc Harper and get him to give your aunt an injec-
tion."

But Tina wasn't satisfied with the way things had gone.

"Link didn't do it either," she insisted. "He didn't! He
didn't!"

"No," her father said sarcastically as he dialed. "It was
the fairy queen."

"I know who did it!" Tina said. "I'm sure I do."

"So do I," Link said grimly. "And by the Lord Harry,
when I catch up with him, he'll get more than octopuses
up his basket."

"Hullo," said Mr. Banks on the phone. "Is that Doctor
Harper?"

"Hullo," said a voice at the back door. "Is that Link
Banks?"

It was Bob Joy, looking for a passenger.

8

The trip out to the rig in the helicopter wasn't as exciting as it should have been. Link was still too stirred up to enjoy it. His farewell had been dreadful—Tina in tears, his father stern and stony, Aunt Jessica still sobbing in the bedroom. And so, when the helicopter lifted off and swung out over the bay, Link sat staring in front of him, seeing Aunt Jessica reeling about hysterically with the octopus hanging from her arm, instead of enjoying the wide sweep of the headlands and the coast.

It was all the worse because the day was perfect—not a cloud in the sky, and the sea like a kitten purring. It was a picture-book morning. Inland, the cows stood in their pastures like Noah's Ark animals, the dunes shone in the sunshine, the seabirds swarmed along the shore in clouds of white confetti.

"Lovely day," Bob Joy called above the chopping and shushing of the rotor blades.

Link woke up. "What's that?"

"Beaut day."

"Uh-huh. Yes, I guess it is."

It wasn't until the rig loomed up below them that Link came out of himself and realized what an important moment in his life this really was. He sat forward and peered down intently, his nose almost touching the sides of the bubble enclosing him.

"Jeepers!" he said.

"Some rig, huh?" Bob Joy yelled.

"Fantastic." It was an incredible sight. The water was so calm and clear that Link could see *Explorer King*'s stupendous feet submerged far below, like the gray shadows of lurking submarines, and the six huge legs rising from them until they broke clear of the water and reared up to support the deck.

"Iceberg principle," Bob Joy yelled. "You can see how much of her is under the water."

"Yes."

"Take a bit to shift her—down in the water like that."

"Yes."

"One of the best rigs in the business."

"I guess."

"Ought to be—cost twenty millions."

They seemed to be looking straight down on the deck now, with its great maze of gear—masses of stacked drill pipe, hydraulic lines and hoses, draw works, cement pods and mud tanks, motors, cables, ropes, chains, and every kind of tackle. And rising spare and ribbed above it all, the towering derrick.

The helicopter spun around it sharply, almost as if it was fixed to the tower by a rubber band, and then began descending gently toward the landing pad—a small metal square stuck out beyond the edge of the rig, and painted with bright orange and white circles, like an archer's target. It seemed perilously tiny, thrust out like that over the sea, but Bob Joy was as unconcerned as if he was sitting himself down in an easy chair. He was whistling "Waltzing Matilda" and giving the thumbs-up sign to a couple of men working at the drilling table. When they were within a meter of the pad he steadied the descent, and they seemed to hover there in the air for a second or two as if the helicopter was making quite certain it wasn't going to sit down on a bed of prickles or a slab of jelly. Then it dropped softly and came to rest, rocking gently as the rotor slowed to a stop.

"Welcome aboard."

They had barely opened the doors and stepped out before Mr. Huxtable was climbing the low stairway up to the pad, calling greetings. He strode across to Link, holding out his hand.

"Glad you could make it."

"Thanks, Mr. Huxtable."

"Call me Brent."

"Thanks, Mr. . . . Brent."

He turned to Bob Joy. "Good trip, Bob? Everything okay with young Charlie?"

"Snug in hospital. They're setting his arm in plaster. He'll be back in a couple of weeks."

"Good! Good!"

Mr. Huxtable beamed. "Quick work, eh? Nine o'clock we lose one guy, eleven o'clock we got ourselves a new one." He slapped Link's back. "Right this way, Link. I'll take you to The Sausage and introduce you."

Bob saw the look on Link's face. "The head cook," he explained. "The Sausage."

Link smiled uncertainly. "Because that's what he serves?"

Mr. Huxtable roared. "Because his name sounds like

one—frying. I can never remember it myself. What is it again, Bob?"

"Sossauvsky. Rudolf Sossauvsky. Written with an 'au' but pronounced Sossoffsky."

"That's it, that's it," said Mr. Huxtable. "But none of the crew know it. It's simply The Sausage, and always will be."

"And a good cook," Bob Joy said.

"You're right, Bob. A damn fine cook."

They picked their way across the deck toward the stairs that led to the living quarters. The drilling crew was hard at work and Link gawked, fascinated. Mr. Huxtable saw him and paused.

"Ever been on a rig before, Link?"

"Never."

"New experience, huh?"

"Incredible."

Link looked around him. Now that he could see everything at close quarters, it all seemed more unbelievable than ever. And the size staggered him.

"It's even bigger than it looks," he said lamely. "Like an island."

"So it is in a way. A man-made island."

"I'll never understand all the detail," Link said.

"It's a mighty complicated operation," Mr. Huxtable answered jovially. "And mighty costly, yes sir."

Three men were busy at the drill pipe, and a fourth man operated a big winding drum coiled thick with steel cable. A fifth man stood on a deck high up in the derrick.

"That's a drilling team—five men," said Mr. Huxtable.

"The man on the brake and drum is the driller, his three assistants are the roughnecks, and the guy up top is the derrick man. Then there's another fellow who gives the orders—called a tool pusher."

"What are they doing now?" Link asked.

"They're coming out of the hole."

"They're what?" Link's bewilderment showed in his face.

Bob Joy laughed uproariously. "You'll get used to the language, Link. It means they're pulling up the drill pipe."

Mr. Huxtable laughed too. "I doubt whether men could come out of the hole," he said; "though sometimes the drillers'll swear that little men do—gremlins and green people and suchlike who louse up the works."

"Why are they pulling up the pipe?" Link asked, sticking to language he understood.

Mr. Huxtable could see that Link was already fascinated by what was going on.

"Why don't we just stay here and watch?" he said. "The Sausage can wait."

"He doesn't know Link's coming, does he?" Bob asked.

"I told him. But Link doesn't start officially till twelve o'clock."

They all stood silently and watched for a while. To Link, struggling to acclimatize himself, it seemed quite unreal. The sea around him, the bold dark line of the coast to the north, the huge arch of the sky, the bright sunshine, the blue ripple-marked water—and here on this island of steel the hum of machinery, the clank of metal, and the voices of men.

"You've got to come out of the hole for lots of reasons," said Mr. Huxtable. "Maybe to replace a worn bit, or take a core, or run a drill-stem test, or whatever."

"Yes," Link answered, not very much the wiser.

"And you can't just pull the drill pipe out and leave it sticking up in the air," Bob Joy added; "not when there's a couple of kilometers of it."

Link had never really thought about that before.

"So we have to break the pipe into sections." Mr. Huxtable made the final point. "And that's what this crew is doing right now."

Link marveled at the efficiency of the men. They looked as if they could have done it in their sleep. The drum spun around, the steel rope moved smoothly over the pulleys in the blocks up in the derrick, and the big hook pulled the drill pipe swiftly into view.

"Now, that steel thing with hinges and jaws that's grabbing the pipe," Bob said, "that's the slips."

"The slips," Link repeated mechanically.

"A set of slips. It holds on to the pipe like an alligator, so it doesn't fall back down the hole."

Link saw the point. "There'd be a nice old mess if that happened. You'd have to fish for it."

"It's happened before today," Mr. Huxtable said. "In deeper holes than this one."

A question he'd been wanting to ask for a long time stirred Link. "How deep *is* this one?"

Bob looked at Mr. Huxtable. "How far are we down? Five thousand?"

"Five and a half."

"Meters?" Link asked in amazement.

"Feet! Oilmen are a hard-bitten lot. I doubt they'll change to metrics for a while."

"About a mile," Bob Joy said. "And two more to go."

"Jeepers."

Mr. Huxtable resumed. "They're not halfway out of the hole yet—maybe what you'd call a kilometer still to go."

"It must take an awfully long time," Link said, "just to put the drill pipe in and out of the well."

"Not as long as you think."

"How long?"

"Depends on conditions. But a good crew would come out of ten thousand feet—say three thousand meters—in six hours."

"Unscrewing every length of pipe, piece by piece?"

"Every *stand*. Drill pipe usually comes in thirty-foot lengths, five inches in diameter—that's about nine meters long, and thirteen centimeters thick—but they only break it at every third joint. So they have a piece ninety feet long —just under thirty meters—and that's called a stand. They stand it back in the derrick, in racks, till they're ready to go back down the hole again."

"And they unscrew it right above there?" Link pointed.

"Right, the table above the slips. That joint is called a tool-joint—just a female thread welded into the drill pipe every thirty feet. Those big wrenches are called tongs. They're for holding the pipe while they unscrew it. Then when the joint is loose they just back it off with the table, pick up the ninety-foot piece with the block and tackle, and

96

rack it in the derrick. Then pull up more drill pipe again, and repeat the whole process." Mr. Huxtable stopped to blow his nose. "Simple," said Bob Joy.

Again they watched in silence. Although Link was beginning to get the hang of it, his mind kept picturing that long, long pencil of drill pipe—a kilometer or more of it—hanging down below them in the well. And he kept wondering how on earth they always stopped it from slipping through their clutches like a wet sausage and plummeting back into the narrow darkness. Or, for that matter, how a thin thread of metal like that managed to turn a drilling bit miles below them without breaking into a hundred pieces.

"They make it look easy," Bob said. "How long do you reckon they take to dismantle one stand—from go to whoa?"

Link watched as he thought. "I don't know, five minutes maybe."

"Two minutes."

"Two minutes?"

"Sure. You want to time them?" He thrust his wrist forward and pointed to the second hand on his watch. "Ready? Just wait till they start a new round."

They waited while the derrick man unlatched a stand and racked it away.

"Now!" Bob called. The second hand stuttered urgently around, but the driller and his crew went on with their job unperturbed and unknowing. Down came the traveling block and the hook—or elevator—and latched onto the top of the drill pipe. "Sixteen seconds," called Bob Joy.

Off came the jaws of the slips and up slid another ninety feet of pipe as the elevator hauled on it hard. "Eighty seconds," said Bob.

Mr. Huxtable leaned across and gazed at the watch face too. "Going to be an interesting race," he said, "especially since those guys don't know it's going on."

On went the slips again, gripping the drill pipe fiercely, and the roughnecks slammed in the tongs to break the joint and start unscrewing.

Link was suddenly aware of the kind of men the roughnecks were—their strong wrists and forearms greasy with drilling mud, their boots spattered with it, their yellow helmets dented and dirty.

"Ninety seconds."

"Joint broken," said Mr. Huxtable excitedly. "Backing off now; gathering speed."

"One hundred seconds."

"Joint clear. Elevator picking up the stand and swinging off."

"A hundred and ten seconds."

Mr. Huxtable was switching his gaze from the rig to the watch more and more quickly, his head moving back and forth like that of a spectator at a Ping-Pong match. "My George Washington, it's going to be close."

"A hundred and fifteen seconds."

"Derrick man unlatching the pipe from the elevator. It's going to be neck and neck."

Mr. Huxtable gave a snort of impatience. "Damn, he's flunked it. Hand must have slipped."

"A hundred and twenty seconds. Time's up!"

"The stand is clear. There she goes, racked and ready."

"A hundred and thirty," said Bob. He pulled his sleeve down over his watch. "Not bad going, even if they averaged three minutes for a stand."

"Not when they're doing it hour after hour," said Mr. Huxtable. "Sure gets pretty monotonous, coming out of a deep hole."

"And going back in again, I guess," Link said.

"Sure. Those guys must get mighty sick of tongs and slips and chains. They'd be breaking joints in their sleep, I reckon." Mr. Huxtable started to walk away; he beckoned Link to follow. "I guess we'd better go meet The Sausage, Link. Get you settled in."

Bob moved away too. "I'll leave you to it," he said. "But if there's anything you want, just sing out. I'll be going back to Ripple Bay later in the day."

"Thanks," Link said. "Thanks very much." With a shock he realized that Ripple Bay was already a long way away.

Down in the living quarters everything was modern and comfortable. Link was astonished. Cabins, lockers, bunks with innerspring mattresses, dining and recreation rooms, bathrooms, new furniture, refrigerators, deep-freeze units, air conditioning—and, finally, an ultramodern kitchen of chrome and bright colors, where he met The Sausage.

He was a sausage—a broad cylindrical man, with small arms, a generous moustache, and a hearty round face, forever shining and beaming. At one end of him his head was covered by a rakish beret that made him look like a French bicycle rider, and at the other end his feet were hidden in orange slippers like overdone cocktail frank-furters. His personality was as large and excitable as his looks. And he was never happy unless he was in his kitchen handing out huge meals to the hungry oilmen and bask-ing in their praises.

"So, so," he said. "You are the new Charlie, while Char-lie gets a new arm. Good, good."

"I'm sure you two will get on," Mr. Huxtable said. "I know Link and his father, Mr. Rudolf, and they have my recommendation."

Link smiled inwardly at the realization that Mr. Hux-table didn't want to say "Sausage," yet couldn't remember the cook's right name either.

"No worries, no worries at all. If he do the job, no wor-ries."

"He'll do the job okay."

"Good, Mr. Huxtable. Good, good. We just finish this dinner, then Link can start."

It wasn't until later that Link realized the meaning of "this dinner." On a rig that worked around the clock there were other dinners, of course, some in the early morning and some in the middle of the night.

"No worries," said The Sausage jovially. "I show him good and then he does it good. No worries at all."

And so it was. Link found the work easy. He had always been handy about the kitchen, ever since his mother had died, and he slipped into the routine of the rig without a ripple. It was largely a matter of preparing before meals and cleaning up after: vegetables to chop, soup to stir, cans to open, bread to slice ("mind your fingers in the slicer,

Link, good, good, no worries"), butter and jam to put out on the tables, saltshakers and sugar basins to fill, coffeepots to watch, and the dining room to tidy. And, of course, endless dishes to wash up and dry. He had to work a twelve-hour shift along with most of the men. Twelve hours on and twelve hours off. They preferred to do this on the offshore rigs, working hard for a couple of weeks and then having a week's break on shore where they could visit their families or go on the town in Adelaide or Melbourne. The eight-hour shift of the onshore oilmen, with sixteen hours off each day, wasn't much good out on a platform in the sea.

But Link liked the life. By working from midday to midnight he could go to bed soon after twelve and get up again at seven the next morning. Then he had five hours all to himself to watch the routine of the rig going on about him. He felt very strongly that the next couple of weeks would be the only weeks in his life that he was ever likely to spend on an oil rig, and there was so much to see and learn. He wasn't interested in the recreation room, even though *Explorer King* had wonderful amenities—television sets, a screen and projector for films, card games of all sorts, chess sets, a good collection of books. Anyone who complained of boredom when he was off duty was hard to please.

Link, as The Sausage would have said, had no worries. Even his bed was comfortable—a neat bunk in a tiny two-berth cabin that Charlie normally shared with another hand, who was away on leave just now. So when he'd finished his first shift, he crawled straight in under the sheets, yawned hugely, and curled up to go to sleep. For a while he was strongly aware of the strange world around him—the throb of the big diesel power plant, the clank of metal, the faint quiver of unexplained vibrations. His imagination added to it. In his mind's eye he could see the huge submerged barges buoying up *Explorer King*, the sea washing against the colossal legs below the deck, the winking of the red warning lights high on the derrick. And far below him, on the end of the mile-long string of drill pipe, the bit turning endlessly, its teeth grinding through the rock ruthlessly, relentlessly—deeper down, always deeper down. After a while, the whirling cogs began to mesmerize his eyes, and he fell asleep to a dream of roughnecks drilling a nine-inch hole in his cabin, until they struck a gusher of seawater that spurted up through the floor. But the bit didn't stop. All night long it drilled farther into the heart of the rock, like a living thing full of malice. Deeper down, it seemed to be singing, always deeper down.

9

Link woke early the next morning and went straight up on deck. It was another perfect day—the sky high and wide, the air brisk with sea tang, the young sunlight full of hard bright edges. He stood looking about him for a while and then turned and gazed steadily at the coastline to the north, in the direction of Ripple Bay. As he did so, a strange feeling swept him. It was a feeling of disorientation, of coming unstuck, as if his life had spun through half a circle and everything had been reversed. Instead of being inside Ripple Bay and automatically feeling a part of its doing and thinking, he was suddenly outside it; and the rig, which until now had been on the horizon, aloof, distant, and sinister, was miraculously his home, insuparably a part of himself.

A faint column of thin blue smoke rose from the western headland as he watched: Craypot's mother getting the breakfast, perhaps, or Mr. Hackett's wood stove giving trouble again, first smoking out the kitchen, then burning the bacon. A turmoil of thoughts tumbled through Link's mind. Craypot and Hookie, the townspeople, his father, Tina's gift to Aunt Jessica, the octopus . . . It was all so remote. Although it had happened only yesterday, it seemed like a year ago. Although the place was only a few kilometers across the water, it was half a world away. His attitudes had changed too. The rig was now his floating home. And the crew manning it were ordinary fellows doing a job. He was one of them.

Link stood with his brow puckered, thinking hard. What was happening to him, he wondered. Was he suddenly on the wrong side of the fence?

"A mighty fine sea for an oilman," said a voice behind him. "Gentle as a cradle rocking."

He knew at once who it was. "Yes, Mr. Huxtable. Perfect."

"The kind we like. Hope it holds that way to the bottom of the hole."

"It's the best time of the year—for weather."

"Take your word, Link. Don't want none of those Bass Strait storms we hear about."

"You can say that again. The seas are like the Rocky Mountains in the winter."

"Not that you'd need to worry yourself on *Explorer King*, boy. She's the most stable rig in the whole world. Yes sir."

Having reassured himself that everything was right with the world, Mr. Huxtable had a few words with the drilling crew and then went to have breakfast. Link followed soon afterward.

He found it odd to sit down at the table in such a hard-bitten man's world. Even though he had mixed with men most of his life—in his father's boat shed, on fishing cutters, down at the jetty—he somehow felt that mealtimes were also times for women, for mothers, aunts, and sisters. Despite the fact that he himself usually made the toast at

104

home and his father often fried the eggs, it would have been strange without Aunt Jessica's hand pouring the coffee or Tina's passing the butter.

There was something rough about this world of oil rigs. Rough and tough. Language, movements, attitudes, eating habits. Big boots and lots of clomping and clunking. Big shoulders and chests. Leathery hands and faces. Hairy forearms. About a dozen men were already eating when Link came in for breakfast. They were kidding Frank Cadbury —the second cook—and one of the other hands, who were on duty in the kitchen.

"What's this stuff supposed to be, hey, Choco?"

"Cow-dung pancake."

"Well I asked for scrambled eggs."

"What d'you think this outfit is—the Ritz?"

"Why don't you ask The Sausage for a few clues?"

"Why don't you do everyone a favor and drop yourself down the drill-hole?"

A couple of raw-boned roughnecks looked up as Link sat down. "Good day," one of them said. "You taking over from Charlie?"

"Yes, for a couple of weeks."

"That's sure long enough."

"Maybe." Link didn't know what more to say, so he sat eating silently and self-consciously, while the other man slurped his cereal and mauled his toast with a kind of carnivorous fury.

By the end of the meal Link felt he was already getting to know some of the men. The members of the drilling teams seemed to fit into a pattern. The drillers who spent hour after hour at the brake and drum were quiet, non-speaking fellows with gimlet eyes that didn't miss a thing; the derrick men who unlatched the pipe from the elevator were loud-mouthed and cheerful, perhaps because they had to behave like gibbons up on their perilous perch; and the roughnecks—the floor-hands who worked on the drill pipe with the slips, tongs, and chain—were pretty true to their name. Link felt he would not want to put out his toe for any one of them to step on.

As soon as breakfast was over, he went up on deck again. The worn-out bit, which had been replaced the previous afternoon when the crew had finally hauled it out of the hole, was lying discarded not far from the derrick. Hank Hudson, the tool pusher, and Andy Freeman, the geologist, were squatting beside it, turning it over and over. He had met them the night before, when he was serving dinner with The Sausage. Andy beckoned him over.

"Ever seen a gummy bit before?" he asked. "Good case for a dentist."

Link knelt beside them, fingering it. The teeth on all three cones had been worn down into little stumps.

"I've never seen any kind of bit before," he answered. "But I guess this one's finished."

Hank laughed. "Is it ever." He turned to Andy. "Tungsten carbide from now on. Waste of time with these fellows."

"We're in very hard rock," Andy explained. "Ordinary steel bits take a thrashing."

"And they're too slow," Hank added. "We're down to one meter an hour. No future in that."

"What do you normally do in an hour?"

Andy smiled. "We all wish we could predict it. Varies tremendously. In the mud off the Gulf of Mexico they reckon they did four hundred feet an hour once. And sometimes it takes thirty minutes for a meter." He paused and looked at Hank. "What's a good average, Hank? A hundred feet an hour? Say thirty meters."

"Two feet a minute, I guess. Just over half a meter. That's good drilling."

"And that depends on the bit?" Link asked.

"The bit and the rock." Hank went over to a steel locker, unbolted the door, and took out a shining new bit. "This one goes in the next time we come out of the hole. It's a button bit—those little buttons on the three rotating cones are tungsten carbide. Sometimes they're high-alloy steel. It's a beautiful bit."

Link ran his fingers over the shining metal. "Why don't you use this sort all the time?"

Andy smiled. "Money, money, money. They cost over two thousand dollars each. Some of the teeth-bits don't cost a quarter of that."

"And how long do they last?"

"Not long enough," Hank said.

"How long?"

"Depends on the rock. They say some of these will do a couple of hundred hours. I'm happy if I get fifty."

"And what if the rock is too hard even for these?"

"Some limestone is."

"Well, what then?"

"A diamond bit."

"Diamond!"

"Yes, at ten thousand dollars a pop."

"Wow-ee!"

Hank got up and returned the bit to the locker. Then he went over to talk to the driller.

Because the downward rate was now so slow, it was obvious that the crew was having a quiet time. It would take ten hours of drilling before they would need to add another joint of drill pipe to the string.

Link and Andy sat watching for a while.

"I still don't really understand how it works," Link said. "Especially this mud business."

"Right," said Andy firmly. "Lesson number one coming up."

"Lesson number two," Link said. "I had number one yesterday with Mr. Huxtable."

"From the headmaster himself," Andy said, raising his eyebrows. "And what was the lesson about?"

"About coming out of the drill-hole."

"Well I'm sorry to have to say it, but that's putting the cart before the horse. You have to go into the drill-hole before you can come out of it. Right?"

"Right," said Link.

"Good, so let's start."

Link liked Andy. He was a quiet, slightly built young man, who looked rather like a professor, with thin hands, a mop of sandy hair, and thick gold-rimmed glasses. And he was a good teacher. Within ten minutes he had taken Link methodically over the whole business from start to finish, pointing out each stage right there in front of his eyes: first, the big diesels that supplied the power and turned a heavy circular metal disk a meter or so in diameter, called the drilling table; then the kelly—a hollow pipe thirteen meters long and square or octagonal in shape which slotted into the table; then the drill pipe (or drill-string, as it was called when the pieces of pipe were all fastened together); and last of all, the bit.

"So," Andy said, summing up, "the draw works turn the table, the table turns the kelly, the kelly turns the drill-string, and the drill-string turns the bit." He laughed. "It's something like the anklebone connected to the shinbone, connected to the kneebone . . ."

"That's good," said Link. "But what about the mud?"

"Oh, the mud! Well, the mud does lots of things. It's mainly a special drilling clay from Wyoming, called bentonite. Sometimes, if we want to make it heavier still, perhaps in times of great danger, we mix a lot of barite into it."

"What do you mean—times of great danger?"

"I'll come to that. First, the mud has several jobs to do. It's pumped in under pressure from the mud tank over there, through a special hose into the kelly and so down into the hollow drill pipe. It spurts out in jets through holes in the bit and stirs up the cuttings from the cones at the bottom of the hole. The mud then comes up the annulus—the space between the pipe and the sides of the well—carrying the cuttings with it. They go over some vibrating screens in what's called the shale-shaker, where the mud-fluid drops through and the cuttings are carried away."

Link was amazed, but Andy went straight on. "Naturally the mud lubricates the bit and makes it cut faster, but that's only half the story. The really important thing is that the mud controls the pressure of the oil and gas and keeps it at the bottom of the hole."

"Because the mud's heavy?"

"Yes. It's like a huge vertical plug."

"I've got it." Link could suddenly see things quite clearly. "And if there's a danger of the pressure down below getting too great, you use heavier mud."

"Up to a point. Normal mud is about nine or ten pounds a gallon; heavy mud is fifteen, maybe even twenty. But if you make it too heavy you start gumming everything up. In any case, you need seventy sacks of barite to increase the weight in a hundred barrels of mud by one pound a gallon. So you try to have the mud at just the right weight —not too low, not too high—to keep the pressure under control."

"And if you make a mistake?"

"If you miscalculate, or pull out too fast, without keeping the mud supply up, or get careless, or fail to read the danger signs . . ."

"Boom!"

"Yes, there could be a blowout."

Link laughed. "Sounds like Dad's car."

"Some car. A big well blowing out comes at you like an earthquake. On land she'd make the sound of a jet plane seem like a peashooter. You'd have to wear earplugs three hundred meters away."

"Jeepers. And what about out at sea—like us?"

"Turns the sea into a volcano, especially if she catches fire."

Link stirred uncomfortably. "I don't think I want to hear any more."

Andy laughed. "Not much to worry about these days. They've always got big blowout preventers hooked up, with tremendous valves, so they can shut the well in. And flare lines to bleed away some of the pressure, if they have to."

"All the same," Link said, "things do go wrong sometimes."

"Sure, things do go wrong. But not often."

Link looked about for a second in a fidgety sort of way. "Where's the blowout preventer on *Explorer King*?"

"It's not on her, it's underneath."

"Where? Not in the legs or barges?" Link asked in alarm.

"On the floor of the sea."

"You're kidding!"

"Never more serious in my life."

"What, under all this water? Who's going to know whether it's working or not?"

Andy chuckled. "You've got a long way to go, Link, before they make you Number One."

"I'm happy aboveground, thanks. Or at least above water."

Andy stood up. "You'll have to see a proper diagram," he said. "I've got one in the lab. Offshore drilling is a different kettle of fish from doing it on dry land."

"So I can see," Link said, waving his arms at the huge juggernaut around him.

Andy walked on ahead of him. "The landing base, wellhead, and blowout preventer are down on the ocean floor. Massive. Enormous. The stack alone weighs sixty tons and costs nearly half a million dollars. And a whole series of lines runs down like arteries from the rig—guidelines, conduit, piping."

"That's the part I don't understand," Link said.

"Well, first there's the marine-riser—a pipe from the top of the blowout preventer to the rig. It's really an extension of the well, so that the drilling mud, cuttings, and whatnot can come back up. Then there are choke-lines and kill-lines—high-pressure pipes to the blowout preventer from the rig, to control pressure buildups or 'kicks' when the well could easily blow. And there are hydraulic lines to close valves and gates by remote control, and lines to guide television cameras; even lines to guide the drill pipe itself into the well if the marine-riser is not in place."

"You'd think the stuff would break up in rough weather."

"It's all right while it's under the water, but when it reaches the surface the waves can be tough. Especially in a big storm."

"But there's movement all the time. You'd think the drill pipe would snap."

"There's a telescopic joint at the top of the marine-riser that copes with the rise and fall of the rig. And all the pipes and cables are kept taut constantly by automatic counterweights and pneumatic rams. It's a shrewd piece of work, Link, this monster. Very clever technology."

"Too shrewd for me," Link answered. "I'll take your word for it."

Andy laughed good-naturedly. "Anyway, come down into the lab. It's a lot easier with diagrams."

The geologist's laboratory was housed in a kind of half deck not far from the drill. As soon as Link entered it, he could see that it was a treasure house of seismic charts and maps, colored cross sections of rock strata, instrument logs, automatic pen recordings, printouts, chemical analyses, conversion scales, and the most marvelous rows of core samples that looked like long cylindrical rainbow cakes. On the walls there were also sheets of graph paper with curves and arcs, some in color and some in black, and in one corner a large map of southeastern Australia, showing Bass Strait and Tasmania, with a fair slab of Victoria and South Australia to the north. It was pockmarked with colored pins in red, blue, and green like some general's plan of a grand military attack.

"Who's winning?" Link asked with a grin.

"Huxtable's horses," Andy answered, laughing. "They are the ones galloping along in green—in the middle of Bass Strait."

"And where are we?"

Andy pointed with a pencil. "Right there—not far from the border between South Australia and Victoria."

Link looked intently. "Ripple Bay isn't even marked," he said disgustedly. "What a crummy map. I can't even see the coastline properly."

"The coast doesn't mean much either. Not this one at any rate. We're more interested in the coasts of long ago. The ones far beneath us."

"How long ago?"

"Let's say a hundred million, give or take a bit."

"A hundred million what—years?"

"Yes, years."

"A hundred million years? You're having me on."

"Not a bit. The Cretaceous Period, that's what it was—geologically speaking. Just after the age of the big dinosaurs."

"How do you know?"

"By reading the rocks."

"Stagger me."

"Deep down below us there are thick sediments from that time. They're in basins with other rocks on top of them."

"And you reckon there's oil in the basins?"

"We hope so."

Link looked at Andy quizzically. "Are you really sure?"

Andy smiled. "In this business you're never sure until the oil is in the barrel. But the oil company must think there's a chance, or it wouldn't be spending over a million dollars to find out."

"The signs are good, d'you reckon?"

"The signs are tricky. Especially here."

"Why?"

"There's been a lot of faulting—the rock layers have cracked and moved up and down all over the place. Things have got pretty complicated down below. That's why I'm here; I'm supposed to map it and read it as we go down—piece it all together."

"Wouldn't the oil have been lost up the cracks—if there was any there in the first place?"

"Quite likely. On the other hand it could have been trapped against a fault line, with blocking rocks above and below."

"That's what you hope?"

114

"That's what the oil company hopes. Or that the oil is held there in some kind of trap. There are lots of different kinds."

"With gas above the oil?" Link remembered a bit from a lesson at school.

"Usually. Sometimes only gas. Sometimes gas and water. Or gas, oil, and water. Or only oil. Depends where the well taps the basin. You can draw a chart later on, when you know the field, and show exactly the spot where the drill went in. But that's afterward. Beforehand you're in the dark."

"And you're in the dark now?"

"Are we ever. This one's a real wildcat."

Link could have stayed in the laboratory happily all day, but after a while Andy looked at his watch. "When's your next shift?" he asked. "Twelve o'clock?"

Link looked up from a chart he was studying. It was a diagram of vertical rock strata drawn in different colors and labeled with strange names—Pliocene basalt, Miocene Shelfal limestone, neritic mudstone, marine siltstone, ferruginous sandstone, Tertiary quartzose, Lower Cretaceous graywackes, Jurassic schists . . . "Yes, twelve o'clock," he answered.

"Well, it's five to twelve now."

Link jumped like a startled rabbit. "Mackerel! The Sausage will be gunning for me." He rushed from the lab, raced across the deck, and shot down to his cabin for the special cook's apron he was supposed to wear. Then, just in time, he walked sedately toward the kitchen to report to The Sausage. They almost collided in the corridor outside.

"Hoch! Right on time, no?" the big man boomed. "Good, good, no worries." And in they went.

At breakfast the next morning Bob Joy came and sat beside Link. "I'm flying a trip to Ripple Bay later on," he said. "Any messages for your folks?"

A world from the distant past suddenly seemed to eddy past Link like a fog. "Jeepers," he said, half to himself, "I guess I'd better write a letter home."

"Plenty of time before I go," Bob said, "if you want to."

"I'm awful at letters. Wish I could send a postcard."

"So am I." Bob sawed at his bacon. "Maybe we ought to go into the card business: *Greetings from lovely Explorer King Island*. We'd make a fortune from the other guys."

Link's conscience got the better of him. "I'll scribble a note to Tina and Dad," he said. "And to Aunt Jess," he added as an afterthought. "Just to tell them I'm okay."

"Good idea," Bob said. "Let me have it by ten."

He walked over to the urn to get himself another cup of coffee. "Oh, and by the way," he added as he sat down again, "there's another thing." He dropped his voice. "Be careful what you say—about progress."

Link must have gawked at him so dumbly that it was plain he didn't know what Bob was talking about.

"Don't tell tales or let out secrets," Bob said bluntly.

"Oh!" It all dawned on Link. "Gosh, I hadn't thought of that."

Bob blew into his coffee. "Mr. Huxtable will probably have a word with you about it. It doesn't matter so much just now, but later on if we make a strike—lips tight or tongues torn out."

116

Link still wasn't really clear about the reasons. "Rivalry?" he asked. "Spies from other companies?"

"Speculators. Investors. On the Stock Exchange."

"What for?"

"Some people make fortunes on leaks."

"Leaks?"

"Tip-offs. Advance information."

Link saw it all. "Jeepers yes. They buy shares before anyone else knows about it."

Bob laughed. "Do they ever. Then boom, the shares go up like a rocket and hey presto, they're millionaires."

"So mum's the word."

"Tongue tight; trap shut. Till the company makes the official announcement to the Stock Exchange."

"Then there's a stampede?"

"Sometimes. Especially if it's a big strike. But the company has to be careful too. If the announcement is a load of codswallop—if it isn't true, or if everybody's so excited that they have exaggerated it—then there's strife too, believe me. The Government can even step in."

Link finished his toast in silence. "I get the message," he said.

Bob smiled. "The message is to keep the message to yourself."

He got up to leave. "Give me your letter by ten, eh?"

"I will," Link answered. "And no secrets."

The routine life on the rig was moving so smoothly now that Link went back on duty naturally at twelve o'clock, as if he'd been doing it all his life. He'd written a note to Tina with greetings for Aunt Jessica and his father; then he'd spent the rest of the morning on deck again. The drillers were using a button bit now, grinding their way slowly through the marble-hard rock six thousand feet below, and Andy Freeman was bending over his samples and cuttings, muttering about unconformity, crazy fault lines, and steeply dipping strata.

It wasn't until three o'clock in the afternoon that the outside world broke in on Link again, when Bob Joy came clomping down to the kitchen like a postman. "Mailo," he called. "Letter for you, Link."

The Sausage beamed understandingly. "Hoch, a message from a maiden," he crowed. "Good, good. You sit down for a minute and read it, Link, and no worries."

"Thanks," Link said. He went out to a chair in the dining room, sat down, and tore open the envelope. It was from Tina.

Dear Link,

It sounds soppy to say this, but I miss you, kiddo. I keep thinking of you out on that awful thing—I don't know why you took the job, honest. Anyway, it's only for two weeks, and you'll come back so rich you'll be able to treat us all to a double dinner.

Best news is about Craypot and Hookie. I met them down the jetty next day and boy, did I get stuck into them. Zap! They owned up about putting the octopus in the basket, but I said a fat lot of good that'll do Link, who's in the poo with Dad up to his neck, and Aunt Jess still hysterical and everything. Me too, I said. So do you know what? They came up to the house and apologized. Said it was all their fault and you and me didn't know anything, which was only the truth anyway. You should've seen Dad's eyes, like organ stops. You could've knocked 'em off with a stick. But he thanked them for owning up, and then he came to me and said he was sorry and you were too sensible to do a thing like that. And Aunt Jess cried again, but it was a happier sort of crying this time. So everything is pretty right again.

The fishermen are still grizzling about the oil rig. They haven't fixed up the hatch on Bert Thompson's boat yet. John Leckie and Mario Bukovitch are getting up a meeting to try to ban it—the rig I mean. Hope there's no trouble. You better not stay out on that thing too long, they might blow it up.

I had a marvelous time with Piglet last night. Mr. Hackett came too. He's getting that clever, he can do a little dance in a circle for a fish—Piglet I mean, not Mr. Hackett. And he's that fat and strong.

Well anyway, that's about it. I can hear Bob Joy coming. Dad and Aunt Jess send a cheerio. Watch yourself out there, boyo.   Love, Tina.

P.S. Aunt Jess says are you warm enough?

P.P.S. Craypot offered to buy a new sewing basket that had never had an octopus in it.

Tina

When he'd finished reading the letter, Link sat for a while in a kind of daydream. He felt the life of Ripple Bay all around him again, strongly and vividly—Tina, his father,

Aunt Jess, Craypot, Mr. Hackett, Piglet. During the past few days they had faded so far and so fast, yet one letter from Tina was enough to bring them all back. It was as if she had suddenly walked in and was standing beside him. It was strange, this split world of his. The two parts were so close together, yet so far apart. The town was the town and the rig was the rig. And they would never meet. Except in him.

"Good news, Link, eh?" The Sausage called. "No worries?"

Link stood up, beaming. "Good news," he said. "No worries at all."

10

Two days later, when Link came up on deck after breakfast, he found that the drilling crew were coming out of the hole again. They were working on the last two hundred meters of drill pipe, moving as smoothly and efficiently as machines, when Link suddenly gawked and turned to Hank Hudson, the tool pusher, who was standing nearby.

"What's wrong with the drill pipe?" he asked. "Take a look at it."

The drill pipe that was coming up looked as if it had suddenly caught the mumps; it was swollen like a fat neck all around.

Hank Hudson smiled. "Drill-collar, Link. Haven't you seen it before?"

"Drill what?"

"Drill-collar."

Link wrinkled his nose. "Don't tell me it wears a tie."

Hank laughed. "Just a way of getting extra weight at the bottom near the bit; it's thicker and a lot heavier than ordinary drill pipe."

"But why make it heavier? Hasn't the poor old kelly got enough to turn?"

"It's to reduce the torque."

"The what?"

"The torque in the pipe."

Link scratched his head. "Uh-uh!" he said. "Here's something else I haven't got."

"Torque," said Hank, giving both hands a violent twist, as if demonstrating how to screw a chicken's neck. "Torque. Turning force, twisting force."

"Ah. And the drill-collars help?"

"Surely. The collars weigh over a ton for each ten-meter joint, so if you have, say, two hundred meters of collars, then you've got about thirty tons of weight; and that brings the neutral point way down low, so you've got zero torque in your pipe. How could you drill properly otherwise?"

Link laughed. "I'll take your word for it. Without them I suppose the pipe would twist up like a piece of licorice."

"It helps you to drill a straight hole, too. You can drift off to Siberia if you're not careful, and drill a hole shaped like a banana."

That was also a new idea to Link. "How can you tell, for goodness' sake, whether the hole is crooked or not—especially when the well is three or four kilometers deep?"

"No worries, as The Sausage says. Every few hundred meters we pop an instrument down to measure the angle. We try to keep it within two degrees of the vertical."

"What if you can't?"

"In the last resort, we run stabilizers down."

"The things you think of," Link said.

"Unless, of course, we do want a curve in the hole. Some of the Bass Strait systems have twenty-four wells from one platform—like the spokes of a wheel."

They watched in silence for a minute or two while the

last of the stands came up. As they did so, Andy Freeman went over hastily and stood near the driller, waiting for the last piece of drill pipe with the bit.

"Hullo," Link called. "Nice day."

Andy didn't answer. Link flushed a little and tried again. "Good morning."

Andy looked up quickly. "Good day, Link," he said, and then went straight back to his concentration. Link sensed something unusual in the air, especially when he saw Mr. Huxtable and one of the engineers come over too.

"Last stand just coming out," the driller said to them.

Link couldn't help craning forward, although he knew he should keep his distance.

"There she is."

The bit was up at last, covered in a sloppy mess.

"Not much like the clean shine of her before she went in," Hank said to Link. Then he also walked forward to join the knot of men around the rotary table. Link felt very much out of it. He wanted to know what they were up to, why they were clustered around the bit so earnestly, why there was more tension than usual in their voices. But he didn't have the nerve to join them in case of a snub. After all, what was an off-duty, temporary, junior cook's assistant doing up here at all? He ought to be down playing checkers, or sleeping in his bunk.

A long embarrassing time followed, while he just stood there, alone and obvious. But he refused to leave. This was his only chance of really learning firsthand. He wasn't in anyone's way, and he wasn't making himself a nuisance by asking stupid questions. So he waited.

After about ten minutes—although it seemed like hours —the men in the group broke up and activity started again.

Hank began giving orders to the crew, Mr. Huxtable and the engineer disappeared somewhere, and Andy Freeman went back to his cabin. Link hesitated for a while, then followed him.

"Can I come in?" he asked tentatively, "or are you very busy?"

"Hullo, Link; yes, come in, come in," Andy said cordially. "Make yourself at home." He seemed his old self again, although a little more excited than usual.

Link waited until he couldn't stand it any longer, then blurted out his curiosity. "What's up, Andy? What's all the excitement about?"

Andy laughed, although Link wasn't absolutely sure whether he was covering up or not. "Nothing really exciting, Link. We're just going to run a core."

"A long tube of rock—like a log cake?"

"Well if you put it that way. A sample, shall we say? A geological sample."

"From the bottom of the well?"

"Yes."

"How far down is it now?"

"Nearing seven thousand feet. Over two kilometers."

Link waited for more revelations, but nothing came, so he put his suspicions into words himself. "And something interesting has happened?"

Andy was nonchalant, and he sounded genuine. "Not really. All that's happened is that we've drilled through the tough rock and are running into different strata. I have to know what's going on, to plot it accurately."

"You'll be busy, then."

"I will, when the core comes up. But that'll take them a while."

Link suddenly sighed and looked miserable. Andy sensed his mood. "What's up, mate?" he said cheerily. "Come on; copy The Sausage and say, 'good, good, no worries.' "

"Ah it's just that . . . well, I don't think I'll ever get the hang of all this. Not really."

"Cheer up," Andy said. "If you really want to feel miserable, have a look at that." And he tossed Link a fat folio in a leather cover, labeled *An Oil-Drilling Manual: A Brief Outline*. It was so heavy that Link almost dropped it, but he finally got himself settled and started turning the pages.

"Horrendous, eh?" asked Andy mischievously. "How would you like to be hit with that for homework tonight?"

Link was appalled. "It's enough to make you drop dead."

They were silent while Link looked through chapter after chapter. The whole thing was a maze of graphs and mathematical tables, formulae and symbols, diagrams and complex calculations. To Link, who had never been any good at mathematics, it looked like a nightmare of algebra, arithmetic, and trigonometry combined.

"Oil drilling is a science now," Andy said. "Once it was just a matter of hard work and experience. But not anymore."

Link shut the huge book and handed it back. "I'd sooner build boats."

"It gets you in all the same, oil drilling. Any geology does."

"Well," Link admitted, "while I'm about it, I'd like to learn as much as I can."

"Good." Andy got off his stool and went over to one of the cross sections on his charts. "Next lesson coming up. Cementing and reaming."

"Cementing?"

"Cementing. Why are we carrying all those pods of cement? For ballast, do you think, or for stiffening up The Sausage's porridge?"

Link laughed. "Go on, then," he said resignedly, "let's have the story."

And so once more they sat down like student and mop-headed professor, while Andy ran through the whole business of cementing sections of the hole. Circular scratchers like wire spiders to scrape off the mud cake; miles of metal casing for the well; special chemicals to cause different kinds of cement to dry very quickly; plugs, valves, and high-pressure pumps to direct the cement where it was needed between the casing and the walls of the well; good cement work in the upper few thousand feet to give the wellhead strength and stability . . .

"And what if it's a dry hole?" Link interrupted at last. "All that work and money for nothing."

"If it's a dry hole, we have to be more careful than ever. Cement has to be run across the aquifers—the water-bearing beds—to stop water from flowing up into other formations."

126

Link eased himself into a more comfortable position. "I can't see that it's worth it. Drilling on land is fair enough because it's simple"—he saw the look on Andy's face and checked himself—"well, fairly simple. But out at sea where it costs millions of dollars just for one well, why does anyone bother to do it?"

Andy smiled ironically. "Because they've got no choice. The world is running short of oil very fast. Men have to find every pocket of it on the whole planet, no matter whether it's under the sea or under lakes, rivers, gulfs, cities, or deserts. Every drop is going to be as precious as gold."

"But that's mad," Link said. At the back of his mind he began to see things—not very clearly yet—that worried and nagged at him. Things about the world when he, Link, would be thirty or forty years old. "Why don't we save up some of it—for use later on?"

"That's a good idea. But it doesn't work that way. Not with freedom, private enterprise, competition, demand, world markets, and all that."

"I reckon it's crazy all the same. Like a kid busting up everything he's got, just because he's greedy or because he wants to show off to the kids next door."

Andy sat on a stool with his shoulders hunched. He looked more like a wizened old professor than ever. "You're right, Link. Man's mad, quite mad." He gazed out through the open door at a slice of sea that was heaving gently up and down in the distance. "That's why he'll die out one day."

Link pulled a wry face. "Then I suppose some future creature with five eyes will start drilling down to see if we've all turned into oil!"

Andy started work on some samples. "I guess so," he said; "but not before fifty million years."

"People are mad. You'd think they'd wake up to themselves, being so clever and all."

"Clever is not the same as wise."

"That's just it."

"All the same, you can't lump everyone together like cabbages or potatoes. People are also kind, and careful, and generous, and farsighted, and full of imagination."

"I guess some of them are different."

"They're all different—every man jack of them. And they all want to do things their own way. That's the beauty of it, and the terrifying problem."

"You sound like a professor."

"I was one once."

Tina and Mr. Hackett were sitting on a rock near the headland, waiting for Piglet to come in from the sea. It was near sunset and the way across the ripples to the sun was a narrow path trembling with a million mirrors. The evening was calm, and peaceful, and golden. Tina looked at Mr. Hackett shrewdly.

"Some people said you were one. Craypot's mother did."

Mr. Hackett seemed to come back from a deep reverie. His white hair gleamed in the sunlight. "Said I was what?"

"A professor."

"Oh." He laughed gently, but said nothing more.

"Don't you want to be a professor?"

"Not anymore. When I retired I wanted to be an ordinary fellow in a quiet place, where I could read, and study, and write. I had no family to care for. So I looked about for a spot where I could just be myself. That's how I came to Ripple Bay."

"And called yourself Mister?"

"Yes."

They sat looking at the sun's red disk resting on the sea.

"I'm glad you picked Ripple Bay."

Mr. Hackett looked at Tina and there was a flush on his cheek. Perhaps it was from the glow of the sun. "I'm glad too."

The birds were wheeling and screeching about the headlands and the rocky shores in clouds, some flying inland to the lakes and marshes. The air seemed to be bursting with their energy.

Tina drew her knees up to her chin. "I love wild birds," she said.

Mr. Hackett nodded his head thoughtfully. "They're wonderful creatures, many of them. And miracles of design."

Tina was silent for a second. "Yes, I guess they are."

"No man-made thing could ever emulate them," he said quietly. "None could fly, swoop, swim, glide, or dive with such speed, and grace, and beauty."

"They've got such lovely wings. And sharp lively eyes. And fine feathers—as if forever living in air and water makes them clean."

Mr. Hackett nodded. "And free—free in a world of their own choosing."

"I can't understand how people could ever shoot them or harm them."

"Look at that white-breasted cormorant." Mr. Hackett pointed to a rock at the sea's edge, where a long slim bird sat warily.

"That's a shag."

Mr. Hackett chuckled. "A shag on a rock! Shag, cormorant—it doesn't much matter what you call him, he's still the same bird. And he's a beauty, in spite of what people say. Look at that beak. See the curve on the end. And what a lovely arching neck—have you ever seen anything more graceful? And that shining white breast, and strong feet for swimming, and broad tail, and long sweeping wings. Ah yes, he's a beauty all right."

Tina looked at Mr. Hackett carefully for a while to see whether he was needling her. But he was being quite serious.

"I've never thought about a shag like that."

"A cormorant."

"Well, a cormorant then."

"Historically he's famous. In China and Japan he'd hunt for fish with a ring around his neck, so that he couldn't swallow the catch."

Tina's eyes opened wide. "Is that what they used? Shags?"

"Cormorants."

Tina laughed. "I'll get it right soon. It's just that everyone calls them shags. And they always seem to be sitting on rocks."

"Do you know why?"

"No, why?"

"Because their plumage absorbs a lot of water. So after

130

diving and fishing for a while, they have to come ashore and sit with their wings held out to dry."

Again Tina looked at Mr. Hackett sharply, but apart from a twinkle in his eyes he seemed serious.

"Is that so? Really?"

"Of course it is."

"How do you know so much about everything?"

"Not about everything, Tina, I assure you."

"Well, about birds and animals then. Is that what you were a professor in?"

"To some extent, I suppose."

"Zoo . . . something or other."

"Zoology."

"Yes."

"Biology mainly. But I taught some zoology."

They sat in silence again for a while, as the sky flared crimson in the west and the light began to drain away.

"What else do you know?" Tina asked. "Teach me some more."

Mr. Hackett started to speak, but his throat suddenly needed clearing and he had to adjust his glasses. She waited for him to get done with it. But when he didn't speak again she pressed him. "What were you going to say?"

He looked at her strangely. "You know, Tina, in all my life I have never had anyone sit at my feet and say, 'Teach me some more.'"

She smiled. "Well you have now."

"You'll be a scientist one day, Tina."

"I hope so; a bird scientist."

"Yes, an ornithologist."

Mr. Hackett looked all around at the curving coastline, the dun-colored sand hills, and the ridges inshore. Birds were still moving everywhere.

"There goes the Farmer's Friend," he said suddenly. "See him?"

"Is that what they're called?"

"Yes, and rightly. All ibises eat insects—thousands of them. Especially grasshoppers and such. That's a straw-necked ibis. But the white ibis lives here too—in the swamps." Mr. Hackett smiled. "And those fellows up there you know as well as I do," he said, looking up into the sky above them. A great flotilla of pelicans was passing over-head—twenty or thirty of them in line, strung out majes-tically in a long file, heading into the sunset.

"I love pelicans. They're so wise."

"And dignified. And kind. They're called the world's perfect parents, because of the wonderful way they look after their young."

"I've seen the way they keep bringing them food."

"They have to wait a long time for their children to hatch—over five weeks."

For another quarter of an hour they sat there—Tina and Mr. Hackett—like two old scientists discussing the won-ders of the world: skuas and petrels, darters and whimbrels, spindle-legged stilts and black-browed albatrosses. Until the light had almost gone.

"Shh," Tina said suddenly. "Listen."

There was a sousing, splashing noise in the water near the shore, a flippery, fluttery sound, as if a shoal of fish was flapping about in the shallows.

132

"Here he comes."

They both sat quite still, Mr. Hackett straining forward in the gloom.

"There they are."

"Oh yes, I see them."

A few little figures came swimming in toward the shore, stood up quickly as if popping unexpectedly out of nowhere, and then hurried up onto dry land. There was an urgent waddle about their walk, a bustling haste, as if they had been delayed while putting on their bow ties and evening jackets, and had arrived late for the party. They were the fairy penguins.

As the little walkers trundled across the narrow strip of beach to the rocks and cliffs of the shore, Tina gave a brief whistle and called, "Piglet!" Most of the birds skittered forward faster than ever toward the safety of their holes, but one of them paused, as if he'd been pulled up short by a cord.

"Here, Piglet! It's me." Tina stood up and sprang down lightly from the rock.

"It's me, Piglet," she said again reassuringly, and walked forward, making a crooning noise with her tongue. As if finally convinced, the penguin turned and ran helter-skelter over the pebbles toward her.

"Piglet." Tina swept him into her arms and hugged him. "You're a good boy for listening to me. And we've brought you some fish. Four pilchards."

Mr. Hackett came forward with the packet then, and there was a ceremonial fish-eating session in the twilight until the parcel was empty.

"All gone," said Tina, giving her voice a note of finality,

because Piglet's bill was still exploring the paper. She picked him up again so that he could say farewell to Mr. Hackett. Then she clicked her tongue quickly in his ear, gave him a good-bye pat, and set him down on the beach. "Time to go to bed," she said. "Good night, Piglet."

The little penguin stood uncertainly for a second or two, but as soon as they began to walk back toward the rocks, he turned and skittered off. In another moment he was up on his shelf by the cliff, and Tina could just make out another penguin up there with him. It looked as if they were moving their flippers up and down, almost like dancing.

"Five years ago, I wouldn't have believed it," Mr. Hackett said as they walked back briskly along the headland.

"That a fairy penguin could be so tame?"

"Not only that; his whole cycle of behavior, as well as his special relationship with you."

"Why?"

"I didn't think the little blue penguin was normally so gregarious—"

"What's that mean?"

Mr. Hackett pulled himself up, embarrassed. "Fond of moving in groups or colonies."

"They often come in dribs and drabs. And some stay in their burrows when the others go out."

Mr. Hackett chuckled suddenly. "That sometimes happens when they're mating. As a matter of fact I think Piglet is beginning a courtship right now. Do you hear that singing sound? What are you going to do when Piglet brings home a wife? Are you going to provide a double quota of fish?"

"Gosh! Dad'll go mad if that happens."

"It'll happen all right, Tina. Just as sure as Fate."

It was a saying she didn't like. It kept repeating itself over and over in her mind as she left Mr. Hackett at his front gate and walked back home. Just as sure as Fate. Just as sure as Fate.

She skirted the big sand hill and trudged down past the inlet and her father's untidy boat shed. The lights of Ripple Bay were shining in the clear evening air, and the windows looked warm and friendly. She hurried on past the causeway of the jetty and plodded up the slope, picturing Aunt Jessica waiting for her in the kitchen with a frown and a sharp word. "Late again, Christina! Don't tell me you've been feeding that smelly penguin again!"

Out at sea the red navigation lights of *Explorer King* were glaring and winking, warning all comers to beware. They seemed stronger and angrier than usual. She stopped for a minute and gazed at them uneasily across the dark water. Why, she wondered, was red always an ominous color, a warning color? Why not orange for a change, or yellow or purple? But there it was, red for danger, as plain as a beacon, fifty meters above the sea, shining down on the deck of *Explorer King*. Just as sure as Fate.

11

It was Saturday—the sixth day of Link's life on *Explorer King*. The calm weather had gone and a brisk wind was blowing in from the south, whipping the whitecaps and flinging a turbulent slop against the great legs of the rig. Link could feel the giant stirring under him, as if half roused and angry at the ocean swell. But the telescopic joints on the marine-riser must have been working well, because drilling went on undisturbed.

Link pulled his coat up to his ears and stood watching as usual. There was a new crew this morning. One of the roughnecks was Niko Barelli, a monster of a man with a body like a tree trunk and arms thicker than logs. He looked as if he could have kept the drill pipe turning with his bare hands even if the draw works had broken down. His mates called him Niko the Barrel.

They drilled steadily all the morning. A hundred times a minute the rotary drilling table spun around like a big flat potter's wheel right at the roughnecks' feet; a hundred times a minute the kelly followed its master, and the drill pipe followed the kelly. And nearly three thousand meters below them the drill-collars spun like flywheels under their enormous weight, and the cones of the bit ground their way downward, always downward.

Periodically, Andy Freeman came out to collect samples

of the cuttings that came up with the drilling mud. He rubbed them clean, peered at them carefully for a while, and then took them back into the laboratory. After the third foray Link followed him.

"Come in," Andy said, "but shut the door after you. It's cold enough to seize up your draw works."

"How's it going?"

"Gently, gently."

"No more excitement? I thought you were onto something yesterday."

"After we broke through the capping rock?"

"The hard layer, whatever it was."

"Yes, it was confusing for a while. But I've worked it out now."

"What was it?"

"Just an abnormal structure. Massive unconformity. Caused by fault movements."

"Beats me how you work it out. How do you know when it's normal and when it isn't?"

"It can be tricky—like detective work. But I'm lucky here."

"Why?"

"Because Bass Strait is already partly explored, and a couple of other holes have been drilled onshore. Albatross One is east of here, and Pelican One and Two are east of that again. It's just a matter of finding out which way the strata have faulted, and how far they've moved, and where."

Link smiled. "Simple. And what then?"

"Then hope for a trap."

137

"With oil in it."

"Millions of barrels. So that the oil company goes crazy and gives us all a bonus."

"And gas too? Like a geyser?"

"If you like. But not *too* much pressure."

Link looked around at the mass of charts, maps, and graphs, and the hundreds of samples everywhere. "I don't get this pressure business. Not really. I don't see why there should be any pressure down there at all—in the drill-hole."

"Of course there's pressure down there. Even the normal increase for water is half a pound per square inch for every foot of depth—.433 pounds per square inch, if you want to be exact. So you can work out what a nice old pressure there'd be at, say, ten thousand feet."

Link had to think slowly, but after a while his eyes started to widen. "Over . . . over four thousand pounds?"

Andy smiled. "Top marks." He waited while Link thought over the idea for a minute. "Two tons per square inch! You wouldn't want to put your toe at the bottom of the well, would you?"

"Is it always as much as that?"

"Sometimes it's more."

"More?"

"You can get zones of over-pressure—where a stronger earth force is pressing down in one spot than another, so that the hydrocarbons are compressed like mad. Then you have very-high-pressure zones."

"And the oil and gas are bottled up down there—like champagne under a great cork of rock?"

"Sometimes. The high temperature and pressure often change liquids into gases; then, when you bring them to

138

the surface, where the pressure is reduced, they change back from a gas into a liquid again."

"Stagger me! What kind of liquid?"

"A sort of oil. It's called condensate."

"For once I can see why."

"And there's usually gas too. Natural gas."

"What sort of gas is it?"

"Methane, most of it. With maybe a bit of ethane, propane, butane, pentane, hexane, and whatnot mixed in."

"Thanks," said Link dryly. "I'll stick to the whatnot." He watched Andy fingering one of the core samples on a bench. "And if there's plenty of gas or oil there, you pipe it away?"

Andy chuckled. "Not quite so fast."

"Why?"

"We get the well ready first. Drill it to the right depth, then come out for the last time—breaking the pipe into ten-meter lengths and stacking it away."

"Sounds very tidy."

"It is. Then we put casing down and get the well ready for production. Last of all we put a Christmas tree on it."

"More weird names," Link said.

"Just a knotty maze of pipes and valves to control the flow."

Link stood up and stretched himself. "And that's the end of that."

"Yes. Just a matter of pipelines to the big storages in the tank farm."

Link pulled a wry face. "What a way to use ordinary words: 'Christmas tree' for steel sausages, 'farm' for a cluster of ugly oil tanks."

Andy looked surprised. "Nothing wrong with that. If this well comes in, you'll probably have a tank farm up on the headland."

Link snorted. "Not if Mr. Hackett or the fishermen have any say. They'd put a bomb under it."

Andy looked nettled. "Big oil companies can be very powerful, Link. They can buy the land they want."

Link flushed. "People can be very powerful too, when they want to."

"People also need fuel in their petrol tanks. So they have to decide—take it or leave it. It's as simple as that."

It seemed as if Andy and Link were heading for their first real argument. Luckily at that moment there were footsteps outside and a cheery face peered in at the door.

"Mailo," a voice yelled. It was Bob Joy. "Letter for you, Link." He came in, waving the letter like Santa Claus. "And some lovely oil magazines for you, Andy." He wrinkled his nose. "Fascinating stuff to read. Affects me like castor oil."

Andy laughed. "Not castor. Crude."

"It still doesn't send me," said Bob as he clumped out again. "And you're lucky to be getting anything at all. I almost dropped the chopper overboard in the wind."

Link barely heard him. He had torn open the letter and was already busily reading. It was from Tina.

Dear Link,

How are you, kiddo? Only another week and you'll be finished on that thing out there, and about time. Thanks for the second note you wrote. You're getting better—nine lines the first time and fifteen the next. I reckon after six

140

*months you'd be filling nearly a page. I said cheers to Dad
and Aunt Jess for you; you're all right with them again
and Aunt Jess has nearly forgiven the octopus, except she
still gets the shakes a bit when she remembers.*

*Well, they had the protest meeting last night in the hall.
Dad wouldn't let me go, but I sneaked in through the sup-
per room. There was such a crowd they didn't notice.
Noise, and smoke, and everyone yelling—it was like the
telly. Mr. Huxtable was there to try to patch things up,
but they didn't give him much of a go.*

*Dad got into it too. The fishermen were saying Bert
Thompson's boat still hadn't been fixed, even after a week,
and Mr. Huxtable said he'd asked Mr. Banks to do it. But
Mario said nobody from Ripple Bay would help the oil
company, and Dad said, "You're the sort of bloke who cuts
off his nose to spite his face." Then it was on. Mario didn't
know what that meant and he yelled out he'd cut off Dad's
nose.*

*Old Otto, and the butcher, and some of the farmers
who sell things to Bob Joy said it was good for trade. You
should have heard the fishermen. They were yelling "sit
down" and "shut up" and waving their arms around. Mr.
Hackett was telling them to calm down, but they couldn't
hear him, and then his pipe got knocked onto the floor
and he was crawling through their legs trying to find it.
He was lucky it wasn't smashed. Anyway they voted at
last, and now John Leckie and Bert Thompson have to go
to Adelaide to give the Government a deputytation or
whatever it is to try to stop the drilling. So you might be
out of a job anyway.*

Oh, one more thing. Piglet might be getting a girlfriend.

Last night, when we fed him, there was this other little penguin there and Mr. Hackett said it's a female. She was hanging around Piglet all the time, just like Tommy Rough drooling over Hookie, and they were both moving their flippers up and down and singing. Mr. Hackett wouldn't believe that they were mating, because fairy penguins start that sort of thing in June and finish laying eggs in November or December. In any case Piglet is only two and a half years old and Mr. Hackett says that's too young. We watched this girlfriend of his all the time, but we couldn't see whether she went with him into his burrow, coz it was too dark. Gosh, if I've got to feed two penguins, and maybe babies as well, Dad'll strangle me. I'll need you, Link, that's for sure.

Look after yourself and make certain you come home on Saturday. I told Bob Joy to see that he brings you back smack on twelve o'clock.

Cheery,
Tina.

Link sat on the stool in Andy's laboratory, holding the letter in his hand and staring blankly at the wall. Again he was back in Ripple Bay, listening to the angry fishermen, clicking his tongue at Piglet, hearing the bump of the boats against the jetty piles and the suck of the sea under their hulls. But it was a long way away. Things were getting clearer all the time, now. There were two worlds—Ripple Bay and *Explorer King*—two empires, two island-states separated by a narrow strait. And they were in a conflict that could only get worse.

Perhaps Tina was right—the sooner everything was finished, the better. Yet if the rig struck oil, that wouldn't be the end of it. In fact it would only be the beginning, because then there would be pipelines ashore, and big tanks, and oil spills, and an endless fight with the townspeople. The only real solution was the failure of the well. A dry hole. Kaput. Then the oilmen would pack up and go away.

But no matter how long he stared at the wall, or how plain the solution was, he could not bring himself to hope for a dry hole. Not when he knew the drilling crews and had seen them struggle and sweat, when he had watched Niko the Barrel clench the slips and tongs in a grip like iron, when he and The Sausage had joked for twelve hours together about the big strike, when he knew how Andy and Hank and Bob and especially Mr. Huxtable were hanging tensely on the result, and how they would yell and dance and throw their hard hats into the air if the well came in. He couldn't wish failure on people who were becoming his friends.

There was no bridging the strait that separated the two worlds, he could see that now. Even a Hercules couldn't bestride it. Little people like Link, who tried to do it, were certain to be torn in halves.

He was daydreaming, conjuring up a huge giant like the Colossus of Rhodes with one foot on *Explorer King* and the other on the beach at Ripple Bay, when the door was flung open and two figures wearing hard hats came clumping in. One was Hank Hudson, and the other an engineer called Eddie Simpson. They went straight to a coil of paper covered with pen recordings from the gas detector.

"D'you make anything of that, Andy?" Hank asked.

Link suddenly tingled with excitement. He knew the gas detector well enough—a clever little instrument that checked the mud as it came back out of the hole. If there was any gas about, it signaled a warning by causing variations of electric current that gave the pen recorder a bad attack of the jitters.

Andy pored over the strip of paper. "I don't think," he said slowly. "Just a jiggle. It's not sustained."

"That's what I thought," Eddie Simpson said.

Hank was obstinate. "What caused it, then? Did old Mother Earth give a whistle or a belch?"

"Bad breath, I expect," Eddie said, grinning.

"Are you sure you didn't knock the detector?" Andy asked.

"What, kick it or something? Not likely."

"Can't see how it can be gas," Andy said. "Not a blip like that."

They all stood eyeing the paper record for a while, undecided. Link thought it was a good time to join the conversation without intruding. "Is there any way you can check?"

Hank looked up. "Only by running a drill-stem test."

"Not justified yet," said Eddie.

"What's the drilling-rate recorder say?" Andy asked.

"Steady at five minutes a meter—about twelve meters an hour. At three thousand meters."

"How's the bit?"

144

"Getting worn. Have to come out in the morning."

"Why not run a drill-stem test then?" Andy said. "Have a yarn to Mr. Huck."

Hank scratched his ear. "I'll see what he says."

As they both went out Link picked up the pen recordings and stared at the nervous squiggle marks on the paper. "How do you take a drill-stem test?" he asked after a while.

"First you have to be sure that it's worth it," Andy answered tersely. "You can waste a lot of time and money if it isn't." Link could see that he was testy and on edge, so he tried another tack.

"Are we getting near the right spot for gas though—if there's any there?"

"We're coming up to the zone, if that's what you mean."

"So you might run a test in the morning?"

"Even before. Any time from now on, if the signs go up."

"Just one test?"

"Run one every twenty meters, if the gas detector and samples show that there are hydrocarbons down there."

"And how do you actually do it?"

"Come out of the hole, take off the bit, and run in the drill-string with the bottom hundred feet or so perforated."

"What's that mean—holes in it?"

"Slots—so that anything coming into the pipe can go up, if we let it. Then with things called packers and pressure recorders we can measure the pressure in the formation. After that we let it go up the drill pipe to the surface, where we measure the flow of gas. Same with oil. Then we shut it in again and take more pressure readings."

"What for?"

"Well, if it's a very small reservoir, the bleeding off will already have reduced the pressure. With a big reservoir there'll be no drop at all."

"Then what?"

"Come out of the hole, retrieve the recorders, and decide what to do."

"Whether to go on drilling or not?"

"Yes, unless she's a bonanza. Then we run in production casing and turn her into a producing well, as fast as we can."

Link walked over to the door and looked out. "So a drill-stem test is the only way of knowing—of really knowing."

"It's like taking the wrapping from your Christmas present to see what you've got."

"Then I hope you run one in the morning. I want to watch."

"Let's hope you have something worth watching," Andy said.

Link worked hard until midnight and then went straight to bed. Although he was tired he was again aware of mounting tension on the rig. He could feel it everywhere —the way the drillers spoke when they came in to meals, the hurried comings and goings of engineers and executives, the urgent skittering of Bob Joy's helicopter, the consultations and discussions between Hank and Mr. Huck. He finally fell asleep, but he couldn't rest. Queer fragments of dreams lifted him out of his bunk again and again, and left him stranded hopelessly in weird predicaments. Once he was on top of the derrick, climbing up an endless column of drill pipe that towered up to heaven above his head like Jack's beanstalk. Once he was floundering about in a vast sea of mud, towing a gas detector that was jigging its pen recorder up and down in a frenzy of urgency and warning.

And once, horribly, the sea and the earth beneath him were made of clear glass and he could see through it to a huge flask, a cone-shaped bottle, held fast in the icelike stone far below. At first he couldn't make out what was trapped in the bottle, until suddenly he saw that it was a face, a kind of Genie, evil and crafty and bursting with power. It was grinning and looking up toward the glass stopper that was locking it in. For there, right above it, was the bit from *Explorer King*, drilling nearer and nearer. The closer it came the more the Presence grinned and applauded, waiting for escape.

A terrible fear swept Link. He sensed what the drill was about to release. He tried to shout a warning to Hank and Mr. Huck to stop the drill, but nobody heard. The bit was almost touching the top of the flask; the Genie was thumping the sides till they reverberated hollowly like thunder. Link was beside himself. "Stop!" he yelled. "Stop, stop!" The thumping increased. The bit struck the stopper and ground its way through it. Bright fragments of glass spun from the cones in a flashing shower. The echoes grew and rose up and changed into booming laughter.

"Stop!" Link screamed. "Stop!" The bit broke through. There was a flash of fire and a swirling cloud of smoke, and then a black shadow surged upward and outward, engulfing everything in a fury of chaos and darkness.

Link woke up, clammy with perspiration and weak with terror.

Meanwhile Tina had spent most of Saturday near the headland with Mr. Hackett. They were both in a state of great excitement, especially Mr. Hackett. He had hurried out of bed in the darkness before dawn, swaddled himself in warm clothes, rubber boots, and a sort of Eskimo parka, and crept down to the rocky beach near Piglet's burrow.

By the time Tina joined him, he was crawling about among the rocks, mumbling incredulously and peering into every cranny with bright, bespectacled eyes.

"It's unbelievable," he said, as soon as Tina arrived to join him. "Quite unbelievable."

Tina's eyes were wider than his. "Has she . . . ?" she asked all agog. "Is she still . . . ?"

"All night, I'm certain," Mr. Hackett answered. "Would you believe it? And singing like asses."

"Really?" Tina's cheeks were like shining saucers, as much from joy and amazement as from the cold sea wind. "I can imagine what it must have sounded like."

Mr. Hackett nodded. "Like donkeys braying. Lovesick donkeys."

He took off his spectacles and rubbed the lenses excitedly with his handkerchief. "I would never have credited it. The end of January!" He almost stumbled over a small boulder in his agitation. He turned to Tina again. "I want you to keep careful watch for me, while I go home for a camera and a notebook. We must record this carefully—scientifically."

"I'll keep watch. But they won't come back in the daytime, will they?"

"That's just it," said Mr. Hackett. "Their behavior is so erratic. We must be ready for anything."

He started to hurry off up the tumbled boulders of the cliff, then checked himself and looked back. "It will be very unfortunate if Piglet goes ahead with this," he said, like a father warning a silly son. "We're all going to regret it."

"For goodness' sake, it's not Piglet's fault!" Tina was genuinely offended. "It's that . . . that other creature's."

"It takes two, you know."

"Maybe, but I'll bet she started it."

"Why do you say that?" Mr. Hackett was grinning wryly, as if he was enjoying himself.

"You know Piglet. He's so happy and . . . and trusting."

"I think he's behaving very strangely. Irresponsibly really."

"That's not true." Tina was getting herself into a state. "It's only been during the last day or two. He probably took pity on her; maybe she's a widow or something."

"It could be because he's a pet. His stay with you when you saved his life may have upset his instincts."

Tina wasn't convinced. "Well he's sure upsetting me."

Mr. Hackett resumed his climb and disappeared over the brow of the headland. While he was away, Tina walked along the shore for a while, picking up shells and watching the crabs and little marine creatures in the rock pools left behind by the falling tide. The clouds were sweeping by and the sun was starting to shine again, although the southern swell was still rolling the whitecaps in and flinging the spume over the reefs and skerries. The world felt fresh and newly washed—the beach clean, the sand sparkling in the hollows, the rocks shining with light. It was a feeling Tina loved. She took off her woollen pirate's cap and let the wind marble her cheeks and buffet her streaming hair. Everywhere along the shoreline she could see the marks of other creatures, the signs of comings and goings, the mysterious urgencies of a million little lives—scribbly writings in the sand, the casts of sea worms, the tiny stipples left by a crab's claws as he ran full tilt on tiptoe toward the water. And the marks of birds: the fine, clean toeprints of gulls, the scuffing tracks of penguins hurrying down to the sea in the early dawn. It was a good world to be living in. It made her want to breathe in deep lungfuls of cold sea air, fling her arms wide, and race along the shore like one of God's wild creatures. It made her want to fly.

She looked about her. There was nobody in sight, no sign of human life, except a couple of crayboats sailing far offshore. The joy in life, the surging urge to be herself, swept over her irresistibly. She thrust her pirate's cap inside her blouse, flung up her arms, and raced along the shoreline, heady with air and sunlight. She was all exuberant things combined into one—swallow swooping, penguin skimming the wave-tops, arrowing cormorant in a clean fast dive. Her feet seemed scarcely to touch the tide line; with the wind in her hair she swept around the cove, swerved past boulders, leaped over rocks, went weaving, darting, careering under the line of looming cliffs, until she reached the headland again. Then she slowed down at last and walked back toward the spot for her vigil near Piglet's burrow. The blood was tingling in her cheeks, her heart was racing, her chest was heaving as she drew in great gulps of air.

"Wonderful," said a voice above her. "I've never seen a happier thing in my life."

It was Mr. Hackett, sitting on a rock on the clifftop and beaming like someone who had just been watching one of Nature's fascinating rituals. His eyes were shining and he seemed strangely moved.

Tina was deeply embarrassed. Her face, already rosy and polished by the wind and the rush of her exertion, was flooded with a deeper flush, and she turned away suddenly, hiding her head from his gaze.

He seemed to understand. "Happiness like that is a private thing. I won't mention it again."

He came clunking down the rocky slope toward her, loaded up with implements and food. "Something to keep us going," he said. "If we're staying here till nightfall, we'd better be prepared."

They set up a base and had a morning snack with hot coffee from a thermos. Then they worked methodically through the whole area, checking to see whether any of the burrows still had eggs or chicks in them. It was slow, tiring work. The nests were mainly in hollows in the rock and it was often very hard to see whether it was a penguin residence or not. But Mr. Hackett was well equipped with a strong flashlight and a hand periscope—"So that we can see around corners," he said with a twinkle—and he worked carefully, dividing the cliffs into a grid to avoid missing any nests or counting them twice. By midafternoon they had found eight burrows where birds were still sitting on eggs, and nineteen where they were still feeding chicks. Mr. Hackett was very pleased.

"I would have doubted the eggs, even at this stage, if I hadn't seen them for myself," he said.

"Because the season is so late?"

"Yes. Imagine stupid Piglet—or his mate, at least—wanting to lay eggs at the end of January."

"And that means the chicks will be late."

"Very late. Even the eggs we saw today are probably fully incubated. That takes five weeks. And the chicks need about eight weeks before they're ready to go to sea and fend for themselves. So these fellows will be ready by early April—and that's about the limit."

"But Piglet's chicks won't be."

"Not till May. And that's when the new cycle starts."

They went on with their work for a while longer. Mr. Hackett had taken off his parka, because the sun was warm and bright now. He was wearing a deerstalker cap, and this, with his periscope, pipe, and spectacles, made him look like a rock-climbing version of Sherlock Holmes. Several times Tina doubled up silently in stitches, while he crawled about from one ledge to another like a huge clumsy lizard or lay like a headless body while he pried deep inside a rocky hollow with his periscope and torch. She liked him very much.

"Back to base," he said at last, lying at the entrance to

the last burrow and rubbing a bruised elbow. "I've seen quite enough of *Eudyptula minor* for the moment."

"Is that what he's called?" Tina said. "Do you know, I've lived here all my life and I've never known that." She repeated the name and tasted it on her tongue. "Yes, I like that. It's got a nice sound. But I'm sure to forget it."

"You can still say fairy penguin."

"No, I'll try to remember it. After all, they're the only penguins in Australia, so that's the least I can do."

They went back to their camp and waited for evening to fall. Mr. Hackett wrote up his notes and drew diagrams of the nesting places, marking those where eggs or chicks still remained. As the dusk finally gathered, the penguins started returning to their homes. Tina and Mr. Hackett could hear them yapping to one another like puppies out in the shallows as they came together. Then groups of them started to cross the beach quickly and hurry up the rocks to their hollows.

"Come on, Piglet," Tina said. "Where are you?"

"Perhaps it was just a one-day infatuation," said Mr. Hackett dryly.

"He probably realized what he was doing."

"Unless she has abducted him."

"*Sh-h-h-h.*"

Two penguins had suddenly paused in the middle of a group that was just coming out of the shallow water. By doing that they separated from the rest and stood momentarily by themselves.

"It's Piglet," Tina whispered. "With his mate."

Mr. Hackett was breathing heavily with excitement. "I

think he has sensed that you're here," he said. "Now what is he going to do?"

"He'd come to me, if it weren't for that clinging vine. Why doesn't she get lost?"

The two little birds seemed to overcome their doubts and began hurrying up the beach. Then quite suddenly, as they passed in front of the spot where Tina was crouching, Piglet broke off and ran straight up to her.

"Piglet!" Tina's voice almost broke. "Oh, Piglet."

He nuzzled her for a second as if looking for fish.

"Piglet, you dear little fellow."

Mr. Hackett rummaged hastily in his bag. "Even I thought of you, Piglet," he said. "Look, pilchards."

The penguin took the first two fish, then turned undecidedly toward his mate, as if offering her the opportunity to help herself. She took a step forward, but was too shy to come nearer.

"He's introducing his partner," said Mr. Hackett breathlessly.

"Hullo," Tina said. "What are we going to call you?"

Tina scratched Piglet behind the head the way he always liked, then extended her hand toward his mate. She retreated.

"Come on," Tina coaxed. "We're friends."

But that was as far as things went. Piglet also withdrew and the two penguins skittered up to the rocky ledge near their burrow. There they stood excitedly, lifting their flippers up and down at one another in courtship and ecstasy.

"Well," Mr. Hackett said, gathering up his possessions, "now we know, Tina. They're mating. There's no doubt about it."

She helped him carry the periscope.

"Yes," she said, "but he still loves me. And so will she—after a while."

"They're happy little fellows. And tomorrow is a happy day."

"I hope they have lots of tomorrows."

They were clambering up the rocks to the path above. Darkness was setting in, but the arch of the sky was bold and cloudless. "The change has gone," Mr. Hackett said. "It'll warm up now."

They reached the top and stood panting; the undulating silhouette of the landscape stretched far inland toward the hard edge of the horizon.

"Let's hope it doesn't get too hot," Tina said. "There are always bushfires in February."

"Yes; terrible days to remember."

They walked in silence, lugging their load. Soon they were nearing Mr. Hackett's front gate. "Looks like tomorrow will be a lovely day," he said. "The sort to enjoy."

She helped him inside with his things and then hurried on alone as usual. The town was bright and genial, the sea sprightly, the stars like scattered ice. She felt happy. It was a good world to be living in.

12

Link lay in his bunk for a while without moving. His face was flushed and his forehead damp. But as reality returned and he began to recognize the shapes and sounds of real life again, he realized that someone was thumping on Andy Freeman's cubicle next door.

"Andy!" a voice shouted. "Andy! Wake up!"

Link leaped up, crashing his forehead against the stanchion that buttressed the headboard of his bunk. It rattled his skull, and for a second or two the images of fantasy and fact overlapped.

"Andy! Wake up."

There was an urgency about the voice that fed Link's alarm. He staggered to the light switch, pressed it hard, and stood holding his forehead, while his eyes adjusted to the sudden brightness. Then he wrenched open the door and peered out. Andy emerged from his room, his beard and mop of sandy hair in terrible disarray. He thrust his face within a few centimeters of his tormentor's nose.

"What's up?"

"Drilling rates jumped. Hank said to tell you."

"Jumped? How much?"

"More than double."

"*What!*"

The news seemed to startle Andy's hair more than ever. "When?"

"Few minutes ago."

Andy rushed back to put on his boots and pants. Link did the same, but he left his door open so that he could still hear what was going on.

"What's the time?"

"Four thirty."

Link heard a hissing sound from Andy like a whale blowing. "Might have known it. Only got to bed at three o'clock. Why couldn't it wait?"

His awakener was laconic. "Wells never do. They're like babies." It was Jeff Marsh, roughneck offsider to Niko the Barrel. Both were in Jim Peterson's drilling team.

"Have you told Mr. Huck?"

"He's in at Ripple Bay." Jeff leaned back against the handrail. "So Jim sent me down to get Hank. And now you."

"Has he stopped the drill?"

"Not yet. Waiting for Hank."

"Better stop her."

Link hurried from his cabin, pulling his cap down over his ears. He peered in at Andy's door. "Can I come up too?"

Andy was hastily tangling and untangling bootlaces. "Yes, as long as you keep your cool."

Jeff started to go back to his team. "I'll say you're coming."

"Be there in a second."

Link picked up Andy's hard hat and held it ready.

"Big jump in the drill rate?" he repeated.

"Sounds like it."

"Pretty important?"

"Could be."

Andy grabbed his hat and led the way out to the rig. "May be one of Mother Earth's little secrets; sounds like we've prodded her in the underbelly."

Sunday's dawn was just breaking. The cool morning was moving over the rig, the air sidling through the steel lattice of the derrick, touching the metal with a cold, clean breath. The stars were fading in a high sky, the east paling quickly. But under the rig the shadows were still heavy, the men moving like troglodytes in the pools of yellow light from the night lamps. By the time Andy and Link came up, Jim Peterson had stopped the drill and was deep in discussion with Hank. Eddie Simpson was there too. The roughnecks seemed grateful for the break. They had been on the drilling shift since midnight and looked as if they would welcome a mug of hot coffee and an official announcement that Sunday was a holiday. Niko the Barrel was standing by the rotary table, his arms draped loosely around the drill pipe. They were waiting for the technologists and scientists to make decisions.

"Ought to come out of the hole," Hank said to Andy.

"Sounds like it. What's been coming up?"

"Here are the samples. Hydrocarbons for sure."

Andy examined them quickly. "Drilling rate still up?"

Jim Peterson nodded. "Same."

"Gas detector?"

"Traces."

"Better run a drill-stem test. Soon as we can."

Hank gave the orders. "Okay, you guys. Start coming out of the hole." He gave Niko a prod in his enormous

158

belly. "Come on, Niko, you great vat of fat. Get moving!"

Niko roused himself. "Is not fat. Is muscle."

"Sure, sure. So use some of it to get that drill pipe up." Hank turned to Jim Peterson, the driller, who was standing ready near the draw works. "Watch her, Jim."

The driller's leathery face creased faintly into a cynical smile. "You reckon she's going to kick?"

"I can feel it in my bones."

"Not to worry, man. We're sitting on her real hard."

Hank went off with Andy and Link to the laboratory. Andy's hair was still in a state of shock as he peered excitedly through a microscope at fragments of the cuttings that had just come up. Link sat on a stool beside him, fidgeting in even greater excitement.

Andy screwed his head this way and that, hunching his body over his work so completely, it looked as if he was about to crawl down through the eyepiece into the barrel of the microscope.

"Looks good," he said at last. "Looks really good."

Link was in a ferment. "Good sedimentary rock?"

Andy spoke out of the side of his mouth. "Good reservoir rock."

"Oil?" asked Link. "Gas? D'you reckon? Really?"

Andy finally drew his head away and adjusted his glasses. "In this job I never say 'yes'; I only say 'maybe.' "

Link was disappointed. "But it's been 'maybe' all along."

Hank laughed. "That's for sure. But what Andy means is that the 'maybe' is a bit more certain."

"Ahh," said Link. "This business would drive me off my crumpet. Too much waiting around."

Andy turned to Hank. "When will they be out of the hole?"

Hank looked at his watch. "Ten o'clock. Maybe ten thirty."

"Will Mr. Huck be back by then?"

"Better be."

"What's with Ripple Bay? Spends half his time in there."

"Calming down the townspeople. They're a bullheaded lot." Hank turned to Link. "Aren't they, Link?"

"If you rile them up," Link answered.

Andy stood up, stretched, and yawned enormously.

"I'm going down for some coffee. Haven't had any sleep for two days."

Hank smiled. "That's not what Jeff Marsh says. He reckons you were snoring like a volcano."

Andy was curt. "The one time I did get to bed—for an hour—he comes hollering at my door."

When they came out of the laboratory daybreak was moving over the world. The eastern horizon trembled with sunrise—a sharp brightness that quivered for a while like white fire, until the sky grew warmer and gold began to mellow its edges. Then a sliver of the sun's rim broke free of the sea, and long horizontal rays darted at their eyes like arrows.

Hank took a deep breath. "A beautiful day."

He bent his arms at the elbows and pressed his chest with his hands. "A Sunday morning sort of day. A church-bell day."

Andy ran his hands through his willy-willy hair. "Aren't we poetic this morning? 'Sunday Morning Rhapsody'—lyrics by Hank Hudson."

The duty crew was busy now, pulling out. They had just uncoupled a stand of drill pipe and the derrick man was racking it away. Link watched him, looking up even beyond the safety platform, up the rearing tower of steel lattice to the very top of the derrick itself. He had never seen it so clearly for what it was—spare, and strong, and sharply outlined in a perfect kind of geometry. The sun streamed through its latticework, gilding the eastern edges of the crossbars and touching the uprights with sudden warmth.

Hank the tool pusher and Andy Freeman paused beside Link, and all three of them stood looking up in silence. Bits of blue sky shone through the open spaces of the framework, and the light ran along the angles of steel in an interplay of shadow and brightness.

"Beautiful," said Hank. "A tower to heaven."

"Erected," Andy said ironically, "to the god Oil and his half brother, Mammon."

Jim Peterson, the driller, eased the brake off the draw works, the drum spun around, and the steel cable raced through the sheaves high in the blocks above. The traveling block and its big hook dropped down quickly to latch onto the next stand; then the weight of hundreds of tons of pipe and drilling collars hung crushingly on the crown block while the steel rope strained through the pulleys and, despite the load, hauled the drill-string after it. At ninety feet the next tool-joint came up, the slips went in, and Niko the Barrel swung the tongs as if he was breaking a tree in two.

"Steady out of the hole," called Hank uneasily. "Keep the mud up to her."

"We're watching her," Jim answered, a little testily. "We can't be more careful than we are."

"Okay! Okay!" Hank stood watching critically for a few seconds longer before he moved off.

"I think I'll have me some coffee too," he said, and followed Andy and Link to the kitchen.

The drill crew worked steadily rather than hastily. They knew only too well the dangers of coming out too fast from a deep hole, especially if there was gas about. It left them open to a kick, the possibility that the mud wasn't up to the hole. And that had all kinds of implications.

By seven o'clock they were almost halfway out, by nine o'clock more than three-quarters. They were getting tired —even the iron arms of Niko the Barrel were moving with less certainty now. But after nine hours at the drilling table what could anyone expect?

At half past nine Jeff Marsh nudged Niko and jerked his head in the direction of the coastline.

"Here comes the dragonfly."

Niko looked up for a moment, then clenched his teeth as he wrenched the tongs. "Back from the pub, no?"

"I reckon. Bob Joy and Mr. Huck."

The helicopter glinted in the sun. Jim Peterson's eyes didn't move from the tool-joint they were breaking, but his lips formed in a faint grin. "Didn't stay to church this morning."

Jeff Marsh eased away the stand as the hook lifted it off. "Just in time for the stem test."

"Yes. And he won't be happy if Hank and Andy have made the wrong decision."

"If she's just soft and dry?"

"Yes."

Link heard the helicopter returning. He had finished his breakfast and was coming up to see if Andy was working in the laboratory again. He stood and watched it circle the rig with its usual little skitter, and then steady itself for the drop down to the pad. He admired its maneuverability; pilots like Bob made it all look so easy.

Everybody else on deck was probably watching it too, except Andy and the drill crew. Bob was giving the thumbs-up sign as usual. He had the rotor racing—a big bird flapping hard to make a gentle landing.

Because of the distraction caused by the helicopter, nobody heard the yell from Andy and Sid Bishop, the third roughneck in the drilling team.

"Gas! Jim, gas!"

The helicopter was thirty feet up, centering itself above the circular target rings on the pad.

"Jim! The gas detector."

The message reached Jim Peterson. There was no need for him to see the recording pen going into a wild stutter of alarm, or to wait for Sid to sound a siren.

"Hold it!" he yelled to Jeff and Niko, jamming on the brake. "Gas."

The helicopter was down to six meters, the rush of air from its big blades swirling onto the deck.

"Hank," he shouted, looking around for the tool pusher. "We need the mud weight up."

In spite of the noise from the rotors, Hank heard the cry and came rushing over.

"Look at the gas detector!" Jim had the words out even before Hank had time to ask questions.

"Stop the pullout!" Hank shouted. "Watch that pump."

Bob Joy gave the engine a last sharp burst and dropped down onto the pad; the noisy racket subsided into the chomping swish of the blades.

"She's spitting! The mud's spitting!"

Jeff Marsh leaped in alarm, pointing to the returning mud, which suddenly started spurting up in jets like thin gruel.

Link caught the last few words of Jeff's cry, and their meaning drove home. He had been standing so engrossed in Bob Joy's return that he was not even aware of what had gone on. But now he was stung into instant realization of it.

"Blowout preventer!"

Hank's voice rang in the sudden silence of the dying rotors like an old sea-captain's megaphone. "Close the blowout preventer!"

Mr. Huxtable was just stepping out of the helicopter cabin when Hank's words reached his ears. They had an astonishing effect.

"Blowout preventer?" he yelled, swinging around with one leg still inside the cabin so that he almost plaited himself up. *"Blowout preventer?"*

The mud was spurting wildly now, gobbets of it flying

up and flopping back with the consistency of boiling pea soup.

"Step on it!" Hank shouted.

Jim and Jeff Marsh leaped to the control lines that ran down to the colossal preventer-stack on the seafloor.

"Shut her in! Shut her in fast."

Mr. Huxtable freed himself and ran across the deck.

"What in blazes is going on?"

Nobody wanted to spend time talking to him about what was obvious, but Hank finally turned his head. "Gas! Big gas!"

Mr. Huxtable was flabbergasted. "When?"

"Just now."

"Are you still in the hole?"

"Nearly out."

"Why?"

"Drill-stem test."

Mr. Huxtable looked critically at Niko the Barrel. "You guys been asleep?"

Niko protested vigorously. "We watch all the time, you ask Jim."

"Then how did it jump you?"

"Too quick, that's all."

Hank had one eye on the mud and the other on Jim and Jeff at the hydraulic controls.

"Tight on that preventer," he said. "Real tight."

"We've closed her in," Jim answered. "Well, I think we have."

Mr. Huxtable recovered from his shock and took over, calling up his men like a frenzied general.

"Come on, you guys. TV cameras on the bottom in a hurry. Have a look at that stack, and check the wellhead."

He spied Link standing nearby in a state of dazed amazement. "Link, down to the quarters—rouse every man jack out of there. On the double."

He turned to Hank, who was back at the high-pressure mud pump. "Stops out, Hank—get that mud weight up." He looked accusingly at Jim Peterson. "What's it been?"

"Nine point two," Jim answered.

Mr. Huxtable rolled his eyes to heaven in disgust. "Fourteen we need. Fifteen, sixteen. Come on, you guys, move! Move! Get that barite into the mud-pods. Weight her up fast. Sixteen pounds to the gallon."

He caught sight of Andy, whose hair was now standing up in greater alarm than ever.

"What's with the hole, Andy? She kicking big?"

"Overpressurized zone, I reckon. Maybe we're through to a high-pressure trap."

"Better watch it then." He turned back to exhort the men. "Come on, you guys; we want to stop this one from blowing her top."

And so the long hard job of building up the mud weight started. Link was in agony over the delay. He was waiting for the drill-stem test and a spectacular announcement of triumph and success. But it wasn't like that at all. Hour after hour the men mixed mud in the big pods to build up the weight. The blowout preventer had closed off the annulus, and the barite being added to the mud was slowly building up its density, until the total column in the well could eventually hold back the gas like a stopper. Eleven o'clock passed, midday, two o'clock. The tension and panic died down, the off-duty men were released, the mud-team worked quietly.

But Link knew that a battle was being fought all the same—a secret savage battle. The high-pressure mud pump was slowly forcing and squeezing the mud back down the well, thrusting it down its throat so to speak, wrestling with the giant invisible force that was trying to escape upward. Little David above was battling huge Goliath below.

And David was winning.

For most of Sunday afternoon Tina helped Mr. Hackett in his study. Mrs. Potter came in for a while from next door with some freshly baked scones, and Craypot followed his mother, carrying a cake.

"Quite an afternoon tea party," Mr. Hackett said, munching scones and pouring tea all around. But Tina could see that he was glad when Mrs. Potter finally left, so that they could get on with their work.

They were plotting every penguin burrow on a map, as the first part of a big project. It was a good time to start. Most of the birds had finished the breeding cycle—five weeks of incubating the eggs, eight weeks feeding the chicks until they were ready to go off and fend for themselves. By now most of the parents were thin and worn out, so they had gone off to sea for six weeks or so to fatten up. When they returned they would be ready to molt—three or four weeks of quiet moping in a burrow without even eating, while all the old feathers dropped out and beautiful new ones took their place. By then they would be very thin again, perhaps only half their original weight, so they would have to go to sea to fatten up once more before the next breeding cycle started in June or July.

"We'll follow the movements of every penguin for a couple of years," Mr. Hackett said enthusiastically. "We'll weigh them and tag them and watch them."

"Especially Piglet," Tina added.

"Even Piglet. And then we'll write an article for everyone to read."

"A little book."

"A research paper."

"With pictures in it?"

"Yes, pictures, and maps, and diagrams."

"Including one of Piglet?"

"If it's scientifically useful. Otherwise not."

Tina pouted. "Of course it will be."

They finished their work at four o'clock and went outside. The afternoon sunlight was golden on the sand hill, the sea breeze nudging the headland like a soft damp snout. They walked slowly toward the cliffs. Suddenly Tina stopped and stood listening. Mr. Hackett stopped too.

"What is it?" he asked.

"I thought I heard something."

"A message on the wind," he said. "That's what they say."

They both waited, tense and alert. But there was nothing. Mr. Hackett moved on. "Where? What kind of a sound?"

"Out there." She nudged her head toward the sea. "A

. . . a thundery sort of sound." She shuddered and hugged herself tightly, her arms across her chest. "I could feel it."

They went on again, but a little way beyond the headland Tina stopped again. "I'm sure there's something," she said. "Just as you said. It's on the wind." This time they paused for a long time, listening intently. "It comes and goes now and again," Tina said slowly, "during lulls in the breeze."

As she spoke she looked across the bay; there were no whitecaps, but the sea was scalloped with restless waves that crinkled and dipped endlessly from the shore to the horizon—except in one place where they were broken by the dark outline of *Explorer King*. Tina seized Mr. Hackett by the arm and pointed.

"Look!" she cried. "Look! Look!"

A white plume seemed to dance momentarily above the sea by the rig—a ghostly will-o'-the-wisp that came and went.

They watched, breathless. The vision dipped and grew, leaped and subsided, according to the heaving undulations of the sea. But it seldom disappeared completely.

"It's constant, whatever it is," Mr. Hackett said. "It's the sea that is causing the flickering."

"My gosh, look at that," said Tina.

A long white column leaped and trembled near the deck of the rig, as if someone was holding up a huge ostrich feather and shaking it in the wind.

She looked at Mr. Hackett in wide-eyed alarm. "Something's happened out there, hasn't it?" she said fearfully. "Something terrible!"

Mr. Hackett was more self-possessed. "Something's happened right enough, I should say; whether it's good or bad I don't know."

But Tina's imagination saw only one thing now. "I must tell Dad," she cried. "Link is out there. I have to tell Dad and Aunt Jessica."

She turned and raced back around the headland, her hair streaming in the wind of her running. She skirted the sand hill, her feet flying over the hard ground beyond it, her heart pumping. Down the slope she flew toward the dip of the inlet, over tussocks and sedges, till the roof of her father's boathouse came into view.

"Dad!" she shouted shrilly. "Dad! Something's gone . . ." She was gulping mouthfuls of air so desperately that she accidentally swallowed the words altogether. "Something's gone wrong . . . on the rig. Something . . . has happened . . . on *Explorer King.*"

13

It all happened within an hour. At two o'clock the pumping program on the rig was working as smoothly as Sunday church bells; at three o'clock everything was chaos and pandemonium.

Link was off duty. Instead of starting work at midday, he had been switched to the night shift by The Sausage, so that he and another roustabout, Lennie Sims, would each have one week working the midnight stint. With a free Sunday afternoon unexpectedly in his hands, Link hardly knew what to do with himself. He thumbed through a few books and magazines in the Recreation Room, switched from one hopeless program to another on the television set, and finally tossed about on his bunk trying to get some sleep. For the first time the oppressive cloud of boredom that the other oilmen always talked about began to close in on him.

At half past two he got up and went on deck again. If nothing else, he could go for a walk around its huge perimeter, measure the helicopter pad, pry into this and that. A Sunday afternoon promenade! As he came out, he saw Mac Dunsire, whose drilling team had taken over at midday, standing near the draw works talking to Mr. Huxtable. Mac was the best driller on the rig—a small, leathery-faced Scotsman who had been torpedoed in the

North Sea, blown up in Palestine, and buried alive in a landslide somewhere beyond the edge of the world, but had carried on as if nothing had happened. All the same, it had left him with a nose for trouble.

"I don't like it, Mr. Huck," Link heard him say.

"Just got to keep going as we are," Mr. Huxtable answered. "Can't see no reason for us to do otherwise."

"We're not getting enough back pressure," Mac said.

"We've only been at it since this morning," said Mr. Huxtable. "Why, some wells I've known we were two days wrestling and hassling, before we got the stopper on the lid."

Mac shook his head. "Something queer about this one. I don't like the feel of her." He took off his helmet and ran his hands through his wiry gray hair. "Maybe she's got a rumble in her belly. Indigestion."

"Just keep sitting on top of her, Mac." Mr. Huxtable waved his hand at the drill pipe. "I think Jim Peterson was just coming up too quickly out of the hole. Maybe he left a few pockets."

Mac Dunsire went back to the mud pump, but Link could see that he wasn't satisfied. He liked Mac—honest, tough, straight-from-the-shoulder—so he put on a hard hat and walked over to him.

"Good day, Link lad," Mac said. "Peeled all the spuds?"

"I'm off duty."

"Lucky boy—Sunday and all. Take your girl for a drive."

"What's wrong with the hole, Mac?"

He wrinkled his leathery face. "*Is* something wrong with the hole? That's the first question."

"But you said. You told Mr. Huxtable."

Mac shrugged his broad shoulders, so that his head seemed to pop down between the shoulder blades like a turtle's. "And you heard what Mr. Huck said. 'Carry on, carry on.'"

"But you think there's something wrong?"

"Not think, Link boy. *Feel.* I'm getting a message in me old Scottish bones."

"Why?"

He threw his head back and laughed. It was a laugh that had a lovely Scottish lilt about it. "You'd better ask me bones."

"But you're uneasy, aren't you?"

"I'm always uneasy. Especially when I'm sitting on top of a kicking well."

"Something could go wrong?"

"Something can always go wrong."

"What for instance?"

He laughed again. "Everything. She can crack the preventer, tear away a valve, snap a flange, blow out through the formation, heave out the whole caboodle—drill pipe and all."

Link's eyes widened. "Not the drill pipe?"

Mac pointed a finger up at the sky, prodding the air for emphasis. "Haven't you ever seen pictures of drill pipe being shot up to heaven like a piece of hollow spaghetti? Hundreds of meters of it going straight up, and then buckling and coming down all over the place—a great crumpled worm of it. Haven't you ever seen that?"

Link backed away. "No! And I don't want to."

"Well it's happened. Oh yes. It's happened all right."

"Garn, it would skewer the rig."

"Sure! Straight up through our bootsoles."

Link looked at him suspiciously. "You're having me on."

"Not on your nellie. You ask anyone on the rig." Mac waved him off. "Go on."

Link moved away, as much to save face as anything else, because he really didn't know whether to believe Mac about the drill pipe. As if reading his thoughts, the Scotsman called out after him. "And this one's got less than a thousand meters of drill pipe at the top, with a bit of cement slurry to hold it in; I could pop it out myself with a good puff."

Although he would never have admitted it to anyone, Link was inwardly hurt. He hated being treated like a kid, baited and made fun of. Yet he wasn't always comfortable being a grown-up either. Even when the men spoke to him as an equal, he often detected a note of condescension, a feeling that they were mentally patting him on the head like a pet. It was different on shore with his father and the fishermen. They had grown up together. The whole town was a kind of unity there, from the youngest baby to the last tottering old man, and one knew where one belonged. But out here on the rig it was like a warship crew or an army; the members were strangers who had been brought together from all over the world to do a job, fight a battle. They were unaware of each other's backgrounds, insensitive to each other's feelings.

Link went over to the far side of the deck and stood

looking out to sea. It was like standing at the edge of a cliff, with the waves chopping and slopping around the base far below. As he did so, he glanced down casually at the water in the lee of the rig, watching the changing pattern of hump and trough, flurry and ripple, as each group of waves rode through on the swell. There were no whitecaps, so the surface was smooth enough, even where it was puckered and rippled with movement. He was about to move away when something caught his eye and he glanced back. There were bubbles on the surface. For a minute they didn't register as anything different from foam or seething spray, until suddenly the thought struck him that none of the waves was breaking and there wasn't any spray. He took a long concentrated look, standing on the very edge of the deck and peering down intently.

The bubbles were always in the same spot and they didn't vary or diminish. They danced and boiled consistently, as if fed from below.

He watched, fascinated. The patch was lively and agitated, as if somone had put Aunt Jessica's electric kettle on the bottom of the sea and set it merrily on the boil. Or opened a gas jet down there.

A gas jet! The truth flashed into Link's head like an explosion. Gas! It was escaping gas. He leaped back as if stung and raced across the deck toward the rig.

"Mr. Huxtable! Hank! Andy!" he yelled. He didn't care who answered, so long as someone got the message and sounded the alert. He tore around the corner of the draw works and collided headlong with Mac Dunsire, who was in the middle of an earnest debate with Hank.

175

"We're not holding her," Mac was saying. "The mud'll come back up at us again if we don't . . ."

Link's hurtling figure knocked out Mac's wind with a *wup*, and took away the rest of the words as well.

"Och! Hell's teeth, man, watch what you're about!"

"Careful Joe!" Hank recoiled too.

"Hoch, Link, is it? What the devil are you . . ."

"Gas!" Link gasped, holding his ribs where he had cannoned into Mac's elbow. "Gas coming up through the sea!"

Hank's face seemed to blanch in the sunlight. "Gas?" He jerked the word out. "You sure?"

Link was pointing across the deck, nodding his head and holding his ribs all at the one time. "Over there! Over there!"

"Over *there?*" Hank looked at him incredulously. "That's nowhere near the well."

He stopped short and his face suddenly seemed to freeze. "God, don't tell me it's coming up through the formation."

They raced across to the edge of the deck and looked down. One glance was enough. Worse still, Link saw that the patch was bigger and more agitated now, the gas rising in a great jostling column, bladders of it, sacs of it, big irregular balloons of it, all leaping to the surface and bursting in a frenzy. The sea for meters around was angry and boiling.

"The Lord will need to be helping us now," said Mac in a low voice, as if reciting a prayer. "No wonder we're not getting back pressure on the well."

They ran back to give the alarm, but before they had

even reached the derrick they met two of the roughnecks catapulting from a hatch near the stairway. "Mac," one of them yelled. "There's gas down below—coming up underneath us. Breaking out around the casing, I reckon—clear of the wellhead."

Within a minute everything was pandemonium. Men came running from all sides—Andy and Eddie, Bob Joy and Jim Peterson, even Niko and the other drilling crews. And towering above them was Mr. Huxtable like an angry sea captain whose ship had run aground. He seemed to see through the situation in a second.

"Bleed her off! Bleed her off!" he shouted. "No alternative now." He turned to a couple of the drillers. "Watch that flare line, you guys. And hope to God she holds."

Eddie went to open the remote-controlled bleeder valve to allow some of the gas to escape. By draining away part of the pressure there might still be hope of containing the well.

"What have we got on the picture tube?" Mr. Huxtable yelled. "Can anyone see what's going on down there?"

Hank had already been checking it. "Not much," he answered. "The gas is threshing and stirring like crazy. But she looks to be blowing round the casing, and maybe from the preventer too."

"From the preventer?"

"Could be a cracked flange or housing; it's hard to see."

"God damn," said Mr. Huxtable in exasperation. "Huck's luck, that's what they call it. If it's raining gold nuggets, I get a bird squirt."

"Stand by," Eddie yelled. "Keep clear of the flare line."

Up to this point Link had not quite grasped what was happening. Although there was urgency and shouting all about him, and an awareness of danger below, there was still no real evidence on deck of the thing they were dealing with. But when Eddie opened the bleeder valve everything was changed in an instant.

A shattering roar broke from the outlet of the flare line at the far edge of the deck. Simultaneously a huge blast of gas and vapor leaped out in a white plume seventy meters long. The noise was deafening. It pummeled his ears and numbed his senses. It was immediately a solid thing—constant, elemental, monstrous—its fury, as it burst from the mouth of the pipe, a living force of unbelievable power.

For an instant everyone stood stunned; then some retreated to a safer distance and one or two started putting cotton plugs into their ears. Link was torn by different emotions. He was afraid, amazed, appalled, fascinated, and moved to admiration, all at once. At last the monster they had been talking about for so long had really appeared. It was leaping and bellowing there in front of his eyes. Link felt the barbarous savagery of it—as if some great force from prehistoric times, chained up and imprisoned for a hundred million years, had burst free at last with savage glee right out of the age of the dinosaurs.

Eddie, Hank, and Mr. Huxtable were running about signaling to one another and checking switch panels and instruments to see how much control they still had over the well. Link turned and saw Andy Freeman standing by himself. His face was white and drawn, and he was staring at the roaring blast from the flare line as if he couldn't believe his eyes. Link went over and put his mouth near Andy's ear. "Even bigger than you expected?"

Andy appeared not to hear him. His lips mouthed something, but Link couldn't understand a word of it. He tried once more. "Big strike?" he shouted at the top of his lungs.

This time Andy turned away toward the laboratory, beckoning Link to follow. As soon as they were inside Andy shut the door and the crashing din was muffled to a dull roar.

"Whew!" Link said. "What a racket!" He was so full of the surprise and enormity of the whole thing that he was inclined to prattle. But Andy was gloomy and withdrawn.

"Is it what you thought it would be?" Link went on eagerly. "A real bonanza?"

Andy looked at him sadly. "It's a closed reservoir— under extreme pressure from faulting. Quite abnormal."

"You were dead right, then. That's exactly what you said it might be."

Andy's hangdog expression didn't change. "It's forced its way into the structure now; into the formation. The surface casing isn't deep enough."

Link understood vaguely. The pressure had forced gas into the upper strata of rock.

"And that's bad?" he asked.

Andy looked at him wearily. "We won't hold it," he said. "We're sitting on top of a volcano. If the casing's too shallow, the whole blowout preventer might go—stack and all."

For the first time since he had been on the rig Link felt a wave of real fear. "And if it does?"

Andy looked out through the panel in the door.

"Subsurface blowout. Plenty of good crews have been lost that way."

"Then what should we do?"

"Only one thing to do—kill it."

"What do you mean, kill it?"

"Choke it. Suffocate it with barite. Bring up big mud tenders with high-pressure pumps, and force it down its gizzard till it strangles. Then seal it and leave it."

Link was aghast. "You mean give up? After all this work?"

Andy nodded. "When it's in the formation. Kill it and leave it. Abandon the hole."

"I'll bet Mr. Huck and the oil company wouldn't agree to that. Not after all the money they've spent."

"They have no choice."

As if in support of Andy's point, a kind of shock wave struck the rig while they were speaking, a rumble like an earthquake at sea. The heavy bulk of *Explorer King*, vast though it was, shuddered and rocked; they both grabbed for handholds to steady themselves.

The roar of the flare line stopped abruptly.

"She's gone!" Andy yelled. "My God, she's gone." He flung open the door and rushed out. Link followed. Men were running everywhere. Some were turning off switches and shutting down motors in accordance with Mr. Huxtable's bellowed instructions. "Shut down! Shut down!" Some were hastening to man the tender that was lying alongside, and still others were hurrying about with personal possessions. The well had finally blown its top, as Hank would have said, and was belching straight up from the floor of the sea.

Link ran onto the deck and stopped short. The whole air seemed to be seething and boiling as if they were in the middle of a vast cauldron.

"Abandon the rig! Abandon the rig!"

Mr. Huxtable stood near the towering legs of the derrick shouting his orders. With all the engines and draw works silent his voice rang strangely over the watery tumult of the maelstrom around him. "Boots off! Walk in your socks! Put down any pieces of metal you've got gently, gently! One spark now and this place will go up like a blast furnace—with all of us in the middle of it."

Link felt cold. Little needles of fear ran down the nape of his neck pricking the skin. His legs moved jerkily, unevenly. "Everyone down the rope ladder to the tender," Mr. Huxtable called. "Then let her drift away from the rig—good and clear away. No motors! When everyone's safe, Bob Joy and I will try to bring out the helicopter if the pad is high and clear enough."

The men lined up. In spite of the danger, they were joking in a self-conscious kind of way.

"Don't let Niko aboard—he'll sink the tender."

"Ever climbed down a rope ladder, Choco? It's easy—just copy your ancestors."

Link almost laughed. He couldn't help liking the men. Anyone would have thought they were catching a bus to a football match, but for a nervous laugh here or a bitten fingernail there. Link stood with Andy, waiting his turn.

"It's a waste, isn't it? All that gas pouring out into the sea."

Andy shuffled forward uneasily in the line. "Yes. That flare line would have been a fly spray by comparison with what's happening now."

"I guess."

"If the seafloor were dry land, there'd be a gusher as thick as a tree trunk spewing a white geyser seventy meters into the air. You'd have to wear ear pads three hundred meters away. As it is we've just got a hell's kitchen down there."

In spite of the cauldron below the rig, Andy's words carried to the waiting men in the tender. There was a pause, and then Jim Peterson's voice came up to them quietly.

"It wouldn't be a white geyser, Andy."

Jim's meaning didn't sink in for a while, till one of the men in the tender saw him lean over, scoop up a handful of seawater, sniff it, and then add casually, "She's getting ready to boil us in oil down here."

"*Oil!*"

The word was like an electric shock.

"You mean she's spewing oil too—as well as gas?"

"She is now."

"Oh God!"

It was the final agony.

"Hurry up, Link! Your turn."

Link hurried forward, swung his leg over the side of the deck, and started climbing down to the tender. And there, while he was suspended in the air like a grub, he saw the fury of the submarine blowout for the first time. As far as he could see, the water under the rig was chaos and tumult. It was being flung up in mounds and hummocks among the huge legs of *Explorer King*; the sea was being torn apart, pummeled, and hurled about like boiling lava in eruption. And with the tumultuous seething and leaping of gas and water came a strange sensation—half tremor, half thunder—as of unbelievable violence unleashed sixty meters below."

Link gritted his teeth and held on. Luckily there was no direct turbulence beneath the tender, and so despite the bucking of the water on the outer perimeter of the cauldron, it rode the sea well and gradually took on its load of passengers. At first the threshing water looked white, but just as Link reached the last rungs of the ladder, a shaft of afternoon sun drove in under the rig and lit up the center of the cauldron. It was the color of a dark bruise, and beyond it were black areas rolling and spreading outward, as if a giant squid was fighting for its life far below and pouring out angry jets of ink.

"Steady, Link boy. That's it." Jim Peterson grabbed Link's arm and swung him clear of the ladder. Andy was already following him, hand over foot.

Ten minutes later everybody was on board except Bob Joy and Mr. Huxtable, who stood peering down at them tensely. "Easy now! No bumps or sparks, or there'll be fireballs shooting sky-high."

The crew eased the tender away gently, very gently, and then, once it was clear of the rig, let it drift slowly inshore on the tide.

"Right, you fellows," Hank said at last, "breathe out carefully, all together."

There was laughter and relief all around, but even then the crew didn't dare start the engines until the tender was a kilometer or more from *Explorer King*. Then they clapped on power and headed straight for Ripple Bay.

Above them, as they neared the coast, Bob Joy's helicopter dipped and flirted in delight at having taken off successfully from the rig without setting everything on fire. It circled the tender once in salute, and raced off toward Victoria as fast as it could go.

The men stood gazing after it.

"What now?" Link asked.

Hank sighed deeply. "The big battle! Men against Albatross Two." He looked back at the rig receding behind them. "Mr. Huck will be flying to Melbourne to phone up troubleshooters from America who know how to handle wells like that; fleets of tenders and barges filled with barite; big pumps; trained squads of men. . . . It could take weeks."

"And what happens to the well after that?"

"Finished."

"After all that trouble?"

"Albatross Two is dangerous now. She's a rogue elephant, a killer. So she has to be put away."

They could see people streaming down from the town toward the jetty, jostling and peering as they came. Link could make out the figures of Tina and her father running at the head of the procession. Behind them the western sunlight was lying brightly on the humps and dips of the landscape and laying a golden path across the bay to the tender, as she plowed toward the landing.

The people on the jetty pointed and chattered, as curious as monkeys. The men on the vessel stood stolidly for the most part, as if carrying a sense of defeat on their shoulders. But they kept their eyes steadfastly on the jetty and its little jostling crowd.

All attention was concentrated inward. The bay was the

center of the universe; the two groups of people were flies on a map. Nobody looked seaward and southward where the deserted colossus of *Explorer King* trembled above the demon it had unleashed. Nobody saw the dark stain that moved near the perimeter of its huge legs—out and back, out and back, with the rocking action of the waves—like a living thing venturing out and feeling its way toward shore.

14

Monday was a day of tempers and tumult. Before daybreak the town was jolted awake by the chomping of helicopters overhead—not only Bob Joy's happy little mosquito, but two black giants with twin rotors that could carry a whole team of men and loads of heavy equipment. They thumped their way across the bay in the early light and circled *Explorer King* carefully and deliberately. They were so long about it that Link, who was standing in his pajamas on the front verandah peering at them through his father's binoculars, thought they were going to wear a track in the sky. The sun came up with light so bright that Link's eyes winced, but still they kept on.

Tina came out to join Link on the verandah. "What are they doing, for heaven's sake?"

"Sizing it up, I guess. Photographing it. Checking."

"They look like big black crows flying above a carcass."

"They are, in a way."

Link had had a happy reunion the night before with Tina, Aunt Jessica, and his father, and had slept in the comfort of his own bed again. The men from the rig had been put up at the hotel overnight, or billeted in private houses. As soon as the oil company could make up its mind, they would either be sent off on leave or used in the fight against Albatross Two.

The big helicopters finished their scrutiny and came flailing back across the bay. People at breakfast ran outside as they passed over the town; the air quivered and the roofs shook with the shock of their passage. Then they followed Bob Joy's little machine to the reserve near the jetty, where all three settled to earth in a turmoil of wind and noise.

They carried the advance guard of the oil-well commandos. Mr. Huxtable had stayed on in Melbourne to organize supplies for the battle—more powerful tenders, mud barges, big pumps, barite, and all kinds of undersea equipment—and to await the arrival of Indigo Ingvarsson, one of America's best troubleshooters, who had helped to control more rogue oil wells than he could remember. Apart from several narrow escapes from incineration, and severe concussion from being hurled into the air above the Sahara by a blowing gas well, he had survived unscathed. He was due to land at Tullamarine Airport in Melbourne, so Bob Joy said, and was to be rushed to Ripple Bay as soon as he arrived.

Meanwhile Eddie Simpson, the engineer, and Hank, the tool pusher, sorted out the men from the rig and cooperated with the leader of the special helicopter task force.

Link was paid off and thanked for his services. The Sausage, who was being sent on leave, seemed genuinely upset and came over especially to say good-bye. "You do a good job, Link, and no worries. Anytime you want to come back on the rig—in Antarctica, maybe, or the Yellow Sea—you just whistle. I fix it up. No worries at all." Tina could have used her eyes for Ping-Pong balls as she watched it all, her feelings a mixture of pride in Link, fascination at the preparations, and fear of the unknown.

Eddie called the men together at the head of the jetty. "We have to move the rig off the hole," he said in a loud clear voice, "and take her out of the way to seaward." There was a murmur among the men. "And the sooner the better, in case the well catches fire. If that happens, you know what it will do to the rig." He paused, collecting his thoughts. "So we'll be walking on eggshells. One spark and it's good night. They want us to bring it off today if we can, but we can't use any of the power plants on board. Too dangerous. So we'll pull her off independently."

There was a swirling eddy of concern and unbelief among the listeners, and cries of "How are we going to do that?"

"First we'll use the tender to lift the sea anchors one by one and carry them as far southward as they'll go. Luckily they're all well clear of the rig, although there are submarine blowouts pretty close to two of them. And while the tender is easing back the anchors, we'll use the old tug to haul off the rig."

"The old tug!"

There was such a hubbub that for a second or two Link himself didn't even understand. He was leaning against the guardrails near the causeway to the jetty, listening to it all and wondering what had happened to his father.

"The old tug! She's a firebox; she'll blow herself sky-high."

"Not if she keeps her distance."

"Yes, down at the South Pole?"

"A kilometer will do. We'll run a towing cable to her from the rig."

"Who's going to do that? Old Nick in an asbestos suit?"

188

"Bob Joy in his helicopter. And the big choppers will be parked up above us in case of emergency."

There was more hubble-bubble among the men, but the comments gradually simmered down to the point where Eddie called for volunteers to man the two vessels. There were plenty of offers. Having sorted them out, Eddie told the rest to stand by. "In any case," he added, as the remaining men sat smiling at the prospect of a lazy holiday on full pay, "there's a mountain of barite on its way here from Adelaide. When it arrives you fellows can unload it."

The smiles disappeared. "Wish I'd volunteered," someone muttered. "I'd sooner go up like a rocket than be buried in barite."

And so the first stage of the onslaught on Albatross Two was set. The crews gathered up their equipment and moved onto the jetty.

And there, suddenly, came confrontation. The way was blocked by an army of fishermen. They stood in a solid body with John Leckie at the head, and Mario Bukovitch and Bert Thompson just behind him, like a couple of corporals. They were frustrated and angry—one glance at their faces showed that. The trip to Adelaide by John and Bert hadn't improved their mood, because the deputation to the Government on behalf of the fishermen had been a complete flop. They'd been sent from one place to another: from the Department of Fisheries to the Department of Agriculture, from the Mines Department to the Ministry of Conservation and Environment, until their feet were sore and their tempers raw. And then, to end it all, they were told that the oil company had a perfectly legal license

189

to drill for oil in its allotted zone, and so there was nothing more to be said. It could drill a hundred wells if it wanted to. That was that.

John Leckie and Bert Thompson had come back at boiling point, with steam ready to blow out of their earholes. And when they told their story, the rest of the fishermen heated up too.

"*A hundred wells!*" John Leckie shouted. "Can you imagine that? And it will happen, if they strike oil. It'll be the end of the fishing industry—and the end of us." There was a volcanic rumbling among his colleagues, and it was decided immediately that if they couldn't get rid of *Explorer King* they would prevent the oil company from using Ripple Bay. The jetty was for fishermen. In the future no one else would be allowed to use it.

So there they stood on Monday morning, blocking the way. The oilmen advanced in a body to within a few meters of them. The fishermen stood firm. The oilmen slowed down and stopped. Both groups eyed one another. Thunder in the air. Silence.

Eddie Simpson, the engineer, spoke first. "Now, fellows, what's the problem?"

John Leckie opened his mouth to speak, but Mario Bukovitch shouted out before he could say a word. "You get the hell outa here!"

There was a rumble of agreement from the fishermen, which gave John Leckie an opening. "We've had a stomachful of outsiders," he said. "From now on the jetty is closed to everyone except fishermen. So is the bay."

Hank gave a snort. "You can't do that. You've got no authority."

Bert Thompson pushed forward. "You try us," he answered belligerently. "We'll show you our authority."

Eddie was getting angry. He knew that his men were listening and waiting for a lead. "This is crazy," he said. "All we want to do is get on board and cast off."

Mario raised his arm and pointed accusingly at the oilmen. "You smash my boat. You smash Bert Thompson's too, but still you don't fix him."

Eddie scoffed. "We said we'd pay compensation. They're minor things. Trivialities."

Mario's blood pressure shot up to danger point. "What you mean—what's this trivy alley tree?"

"It doesn't matter. We'll take care of it."

"You've been saying that for a week," John Leckie called. "And you restrict the fishing fleet, take our berths, muck up the bay."

"That's right," Mario yelled. "Not to go this way, not to go that way."

"So we're giving you notice," Bert Thompson added. "Pack up and get out."

Hank came forward. "Well stand aside then, so we can get on board and shove off."

"Oh no, you don't! Not on the tender; you just turn around and shove off up the road."

Hank was livid. "What do you take us for?"

"For wreckers!" Bert shouted. "For creeps and muck artists."

The two leaders were gradually getting nearer to each other. As one or another of the leaders moved forward in the heat of the argument, so the men behind him closed up in support.

Eddie Simpson sensed the violence that was looming. He tried another tack. "Listen, you fellows, we're only doing a job. If you've got a gripe, why don't you take it to the oil company, not to us?"

But John Leckie scotched that argument. "Listen, Mr. Crude, we've been arguing with your Mister High-and-Mighty Brenton P. Huxtable for a week, and Bert and me walked the streets of Adelaide till we dropped, trying to find the Government. We sat on office chairs till they stuck, and we talked till our tongues seized up in the drought. So now we're finished with talking. We're doing. And what we're doing is pushing your mob right off this jetty. For good. Now."

While he was talking, some of the oilmen started edging their way forward, ready to make a rush for the tender. But Bert saw the move and cut them off.

"Back!" he shouted. "Back, back!"

Almost before anybody was aware of it, Mario had leaped down onto his own boat, which was lying on the opposite side, and reappeared on the jetty with a rifle in his hands.

Everybody froze. Fear ran over the whole crowd like cold quicksilver. The scene was a set piece—a tableau. It held for a hushed moment, fixed and breathless.

"Put that thing down!"

The voice was a roar, a bellow full of outrage and anger. It was so near it seemed like a blast from a loudspeaker, so sudden it took even Mario by surprise. He swung around to face his new antagonist. It was Dave Banks.

Link heard the shout too and recognized it as his father's. He leaped down from the bollard where he had been standing on tiptoe to get a better view of things, and pushed his way urgently through the crowd.

At first only his father's head and torso were visible above the planks of the jetty. He had been working on old *Titan* when the argument had started, and had come hurrying over to try and stop the fracas.

"Put it down," he repeated, pointing impatiently at the rifle. "Put it down! That won't settle anything." He moved forward straight toward Mario. It was a situation Mario hadn't expected, and he backed away.

"Don't interfere!" he cried. "Dave, don't you interfere!"

But Link's father kept on walking. "Don't be stupid," he said. "That'll only make things worse." He paused and held out his hand. "Give it to me, Mario." The men on both sides craned forward fearfully, but Mario didn't respond. Instead he crouched back, clutching the butt of the rifle under his armpit and pointing the muzzle straight at Mr. Banks.

"Careful, Dave," Bert Thompson said in a low voice. "Don't push him too hard."

Link's father gestured gently and held out his hand again. "Come on, Mario."

Anger seemed to flare up in Mario, who felt himself being hemmed in steadily by foes, friends, or peacemakers on all sides. He thrust the rifle forward suddenly several times in a bayonetlike action. "Keep back! Keep back!"

Link burst through the press of bodies just then on the far side of the jetty. In his mind's eye he could see Mario being harried into such a state of trauma that he finally fired blindly at the figures of his own friends. And if that was about to happen, Link thought it was less likely to be triggered off by a boy than by a grown man.

"Let me, Dad," he said quickly, and walked toward Mario. "We're friends."

But he had underestimated the position, for Mario swung on him fiercely and unexpectedly. "You not friend! You help this . . . this *rubbish*." He hissed the word and jerked his head violently in the direction of the oilmen.

Link stopped, suddenly afraid and embarrassed.

Luckily John Leckie sensed the ugly stalemate that was looming and came forward at just the right instant. Mario admired and respected him.

"Better put it down, Mario. Might only lead to trouble."

Even then, there was a tense moment; it was hard for Mario to hand over the rifle, because if he did so he would lose face in front of both groups of men. He looked sullenly from one face to another.

"*Diàvolo*," he said suddenly under his breath and, without another word, turned and leaped down onto his own boat again. It was the only way he could escape without the indignity of handing over the rifle.

A ripple of relief ran over the rest of the men. It had barely passed before Link's father was haranguing the fishermen.

"Now listen," he shouted. "You're not going to stop the oil company by carrying on like a mob of pugs. In any case, it's too late. Every minute you blokes spend griping here on the jetty, that thing out there is spewing more oil and gas into the sea. And you know what that means."

There was a movement among the men, a reluctant murmur of agreement.

Eddie Simpson saw his chance. "That's right," he shouted. "Dave Banks is talking sense. For you as well as for us."

There was more sullen shuffling and muttering, but it was a sign that the blockade was breaking. "That well has to be sealed fast," Dave Banks said. "For our sakes."

The ranks of the fishermen weakened; some began to move back to their boats, others drifted about indecisively. "To hell with it," John Leckie muttered, and turned on his heel.

Hank pushed his way through the opposition then, followed by half a dozen of his colleagues. Eddie turned to thank Link's father. "Thanks, Mr. Banks. If it hadn't been for you . . ."

But the man he was trying to thank was already on his way back to old *Titan*. Link saw him and ran down the jetty in pursuit. "Dad! Dad, I'm coming too."

A quarter of an hour later the tug and the tender slipped their moorings and headed out of the bay. They were the spearhead of a vast task force. Almost unknown to them, many other people in different parts of Australia were gathering up the army that was to reinforce them. In Adelaide orders had gone out for shipment after shipment of barite from the South Australian mines, and already the prime movers, their huge engines howling, were grinding over the Ranges with their heavy loads. In Melbourne messages were flowing for underwater equipment and electronic devices to be airlifted urgently to Ripple Bay. In Bass Strait two of the most powerful tenders in the world, with giant pumps and six big mud-pods apiece, were leaving the drilling platforms which they normally serviced and were racing at high speed toward Ripple Bay. And above the Pacific Ocean, Indigo Ingvarsson was streaking toward Melbourne in a jet plane from America.

It was a massive and complex organization, a bringing together of men and material, of knowledge, and power, and equipment—what Brenton P. Huxtable called an operation in logistics. And the purpose of it all was to make war on Albatross Two: to attack it, battle with it, and conquer it. For suddenly the well that everyone had worked so hard to complete was Public Enemy Number One. The men who had labored to create a servant for mankind had unleashed a monster instead. Signs of its rampage were soon clear enough. *Titan* was less than halfway out to the rig when Link's father called from the wheelhouse. "Come and have a look at this."

Link was talking to Andy Freeman, who had come on board to try to gather more evidence for geological purposes.

"What is it?"

"Come and see."

Link and Andy went up forward, along with three or four of the other men. As they went past the wheelhouse Link's father pointed with a sweep of his hand.

"Look."

"Jeepers."

It was an oil slick, a great black smudge that covered the sea on all sides around *Explorer King* and ran away southeastward in an ominous wedge for a kilometer or more. It was longer than it was broad, but even on the shoreward side it had spread out from the rig for five hundred meters and seemed to be advancing toward them slowly and relentlessly, like some unworldly evil out of science fiction.

"Look at it," Link's father called. "And all in one night."

Andy Freeman eyed the slick professionally. "It's not much," he said, "but it's too much all the same."

"How much?"

"Hard to say. A few hundred barrels a day, maybe. The well's mainly belching gas, but there's just enough oil coming with it to be a terrible nuisance—especially for undersea work."

"Especially for Ripple Bay," Mr. Banks said bitingly.

Andy looked at him sadly. "Yes," he said, "but a thousand barrels a day would be worse than a hundred."

Link smiled ironically. "Yes, ten times worse."

"And a hundred barrels is worse than ten," his father added.

They took the old tug on a wide arc to starboard, but even from that distance the churning of the water from the blowout was clearly visible, like rapids on a river. The men from the task force were busy with their radios, talking to the tender and to the helicopter overhead.

"We're coming up to position now," Link heard one of them say. "You can start cable laying when you're ready."

And so the struggle to haul *Explorer King* out of the man-made maelstrom began. It lasted all day. The tender used the rugged A frame and winch at her stern to lift up the anchors one by one and carry them to seaward, as far as the mooring chains would allow. It was almost a joke to see her nosing about like a big retriever sniffing out a bone that she had buried at sea, and getting ready to scratch it up again. But slowly and methodically she did it.

Meanwhile old *Titan* cringed away from the boiling gas and took up her position a thousand meters to the south. There she waited for hours, until Bob Joy landed back on the rig, attached a heavy towline, and flew a thin hitching line back to the tug. With this the men hauled in the big line and eventually attached it to *Titan*'s towing bollard.

Radio voices crackled tensely then, in a strange triangle.

"Easy now, skipper," the task-force leader said. "Just take up the slack."

Link's father took *Titan* forward gently, gently, until the towline came up hard and taut.

"Fine! Fine! Hold her there!"

More voices crackled and gabbled on the radio.

"All set, Eddie?"

"All clear!"

"Ready above?"

"Roger, take her away."

"Okay, skipper. This time it's for real."

Link stood beside his father. "Slow ahead to full power," said the radio voice.

Titan's great screws gripped the water. Threshing foam leaped up under her stern. She seemed to feel the excitement of her former life again, the challenge of old glories. It was as if she was putting down her shoulders, bracing her body for the greatest haul of her whole life. The towing cable was as taut as a bridge strut.

"Right now!" the radio voice shouted. "Into it! Gun her! Gun her!"

For a minute it seemed that the old tug was going to burst her heart. Her engines strained, her screws thundered, her rivets quivered in the ancient plates. Everyone waited tensely. Seconds seemed like minutes. They were on the brink of disappointment.

"She's coming!"

A shout went up, a cry of jubilation and triumph.

"Keep her going, keep her going!"

But there was no need to urge anymore. Once *Titan* had scored the first notch in her desperate tug-of-war she was not likely to slacken or relax. Centimeter by centimeter she forced her way forward, and far behind her the gigantic bulk of *Explorer King* stirred and wallowed, and finally followed her sluggishly off the well, off the center of the turbulent blowout, out of the milling waters, and so eventually to the comparative calm of the natural sea beyond. There, clear of the danger by more than its own great length, the rig was fixed and held, while the tender tethered it again with its brutish anchors.

"Congratulations," said the radio voice. "Very neat. Two bonus points to everyone."

Bob Joy went in then and wrote the last period to the story by landing on the rig once more with a group of men to stow the towing cable. *Titan* and the tender stood by until he took off safely again and then everybody headed for home.

"Stage One," said Andy Freeman. "The easiest part."

"You can thank the gods for such good weather," Link's father added. "But how much longer is it going to last?"

"Not long enough, you can be sure of that."

"How long do you need—for the well?"

Andy shrugged his thin shoulders. "Who knows? Ten days, two weeks, a month."

Link's father looked at the black stain on the water. "If it's as long as that," he said in a quiet voice, "then God help us all."

They were just rounding the eastern end of the oil slick and heading back on course again when they saw a crayboat sailing out of the bay. The afternoon sun fell full on her deck and lit up the white paintwork.

"Crayboat," said Mr. Banks. "Whose is it, Link?"

Link squinted and shielded his eyes from the sea's mirrors.

"Not sure," he said, "but I think it's *Corfu.*"

"Mario's?" Andy asked, suddenly interested.

"Yes, Mario's."

"What's he up to?"

"Going out to lift his pots I guess."

They all stood watching. But instead of veering away down the coast, the boat came straight on.

"Almost looks as if she's got a message for us," Link's father said. "We'll go and see."

He turned old *Titan* a few points west and set a course to intercept the crayboat.

"He's belting her along," Andy said after a while.

Link laughed. "Mario's always in a hurry."

"He's going to race across our bows at this rate," Mr. Banks said. He brought *Titan* further around still, until she was almost sailing down the edge of the oil slick.

"He'll have to change course soon, or he'll be barging right into the middle of the slick."

"Wouldn't worry Mario."

"Wouldn't worry me either, but the less it's disturbed the better. We don't want to stir it up unnecessarily."

The distance between the two vessels was closing quickly.

Andy watched, puzzled. "What the devil is he up to?"

"Can't make him out," Link's father answered uneasily, "but if he keeps this up he's going to plow straight into the blowout."

Andy jumped forward. "Don't let him do that!"

Mr. Banks clapped on all the speed he could in the hope of pushing the old tug between *Corfu* and the blowout, but she was too slow. In the end he had to swing still further to port to keep his chances alive, and this sent *Titan* plunging into the oil slick. The black swell swept along her sides like sludge, the bow slicing through a sea that suddenly seemed calm, smooth, slicked down.

Link was running up to the bow end, waving his hat and shouting at the top of his lungs. "Back!" he yelled with an angry backward sweep of his arm. "Back! Get back!"

"I still don't see what he's up to," Andy said.

"Proving a point," Link's father answered. "Saving face, defying the enemy—call it what you like. He reckons he's been ordered away from the rig and pushed about for so long that now he's getting his own back. Thumbing his nose at the lot of us."

"But what is he going to do?"

"Just sail through the slick to the rig, I'd say, and then veer off down the coast to his craypots."

"He won't want to get too close to the well. He'll not

only blow himself up, but he'll light an inferno."

Link's father was straining every plate in old *Titan*. "We'll still try to cut him off."

The two vessels were only a hundred meters apart now, racing at right angles to one another.

"Look out you don't collide with him," Andy said anxiously, "or we'll all go to the bottom."

"I can't swing any farther to port," Link's father shouted back above the growing noise of engines and wave wash, "or we'll end up in the middle of the blowout ourselves." It was true. The maneuver to intercept Mario was carrying them into the danger area. He picked up the tug's megaphone and fairly hollered at the top of his voice. "Starboard, Mario. Starboard! There's danger ahead. Gas!"

But the crayboat plowed on unheeding, the name *Corfu* visible on her bows now as plain as a billboard. Link and most of the other men were up forward, shouting and waving. "Swing away! Swing away, you idiot!"

The boats were only fifty meters apart, and dead on a collision course.

"Better give way," Andy called fearfully. "Port! Port!"

"I can't," yelled Mr. Banks, "or we'll go bung into the boiling pot."

Andy shot a glance fearfully over his shoulder. "Look out! There are formation blowouts right beside us."

They were twenty-five meters apart. The men at the bow of the tug started running back toward the wheelhouse. "Look out!" they yelled. "We're going to hit!"

"Maniac!" Link's father ground out the word through terse lips. At the same time he yelled, "Hard astern, hard astern," to Ben Bradshaw at the engines, and swung the wheel furiously to starboard to bring *Titan* around in a tight arc away from the blowout. At that moment, too, Mario at last seemed to realize that his boat was in danger, so he hauled hard on his tiller. But instead of swinging to port, so that the courses of the two vessels might have passed narrowly side by side like two half circles lying inside one another, he also swung hard to starboard, which brought his stern around toward *Titan*'s bow. The tug had far too much way for her to slow up in time. The gap narrowed as the two came together. Ten meters, five meters.

"Hang on!" The cry went up from everyone on the tug. Two meters.

Crash! The bow of old *Titan*, coming around fast on the starboard rudder, caught *Corfu* near the very end of the stern, splintering the woodwork in all directions. Worse still, *Titan*'s bow was just rising like a goring bull in the act of tossing up its horns; there was a hideous grinding as it almost lifted the crayboat out of the water, shattering tiller, rudder lines, propeller shaft, and all. Metal screeched and sparks spat as the blades of the disintegrating propeller clattered against *Titan*'s solid plates.

And then, without warning, the whole world exploded. A sheet of flame seemed to leap out from under the hulls of the boats themselves, and flashed across the sea in the wink of an eye to the center of the main blowout. There it shot upward with a roar into a great pillar of fire, the flames leaping and flailing, thrusting outward and upward, breaking away and returning, darting out to link with the lesser outbreaks, rolling tumultuously in a kind of fire-ball at the heart of the inferno. It was an incredible sight—a column of fire on the water, an endless beacon, a funeral pyre. It was a miracle that the two vessels were not incinerated on the spot. Luckily they had collided on the very edges of the blowout and still had enough way to drift beyond the fiery lake into open water.

For a minute it looked as if *Corfu* was going to sink, but she managed to keep afloat somehow, though wallowing about like a dead duck. They hitched a short towing line to her from old *Titan* and made for the shore as hastily as they could, in case she decided to give up the ghost after all.

Link expected Mario to blow up just as spectacularly as the oil well had—at best demanding full compensation, at worst leaping aboard the tug with his rifle to massacre them all. But he was strangely subdued. He sat on a hatch with his head in his hands and tears in his eyes, blinking and staring in turn at the leaping flames and his near-sinking boat, and then back again at the flames. Perhaps he was genuinely suffering from shock, or perhaps the sight of the fiery inferno with its cliffs and crags of fire suddenly made him realize what would have happened to him if he had kept on sailing bullheadedly into the blowout—like a moth plunging at a blowtorch.

They were just dragging the wreck of his boat into the bay when Link nudged his father and pointed upward. Another helicopter was sweeping overhead in a fast arc.

"Mr. Huck and the troubleshooter," he shouted.

"Yes, and they won't be blessing us much for what's just

happened," Mr. Banks replied grimly. "I'm glad I can't hear what they're thinking."

"Only different ways of boiling you in oil," Andy said.

Actually, for once Mr. Brenton P. Huxtable was sitting quite speechless, looking down at the fury on the water below. Beside him, big blond-headed Indigo Ingvarsson gazed intently through his binoculars, appraising the chaos with an expert eye. When he had finished he, too, sat there without saying a word, while the pilot headed for the shore. Perhaps the task he saw was beyond words.

15

On Thursday the first seabird died. It was a black cormorant. Craypot found it lying half dead on the rocks near the western headland, while he was looking for lost marker buoys. He brought it back to the boat shed to show Tina and Link. The oil slick from Albatross Two was now a huge smudge five kilometers long and two kilometers wide. Its shoreward edge was only a thousand meters from the coast in some places, and it was spreading relentlessly. The lagoon of clear water along the shore was shrinking every day.

Indigo Ingvarsson and the directors of the oil company knew only too well what was happening, and they were working around the clock to try to get Albatross Two by the throat and strangle her. They set up huge floodlights near the jetty so that they could work through the night. They brought in more men and equipment. But in the end only a small group of experts could actually fight the blowout, and it was a long hard job. And very dangerous.

After long analysis and much discussion they decided to drill a relief well, as they called it, which would be controlled so carefully that it would actually meet Albatross Two down near the zone of high-pressure gas. Then heavy mud would be pumped in to seal it off. It was an enormously complex operation. And it would cost a million dollars.

Tina took the cormorant from Craypot, laid it gently on a bench in the boat shed, and started wiping its feathers with a rag. They were covered with oil. Although it was still alive, it was weak and helpless and lay there without struggling; its eyes were blinking open and shut in alarm and its beak kept opening wide in a retching movement.

Tina was almost in tears. "You poor old fellow, you poor old fellow," she kept saying while she wiped and dabbed at its wings and breast. But the cormorant remained limp and listless.

Link and Craypot stood watching.

"I think he's had it," Link said. "No life left in him."

Tina flared up angrily. "That's all very well for you to say."

"Well it's true, isn't it?"

"Yes, and who's to blame? You as much as anyone."

Link was flabbergasted. "Me?"

"Of course, you. You were working out on that . . . that monstrosity."

"Ah, fair go, Tina. I was just a slushy for the cook."

"Doesn't matter. You helped."

"Ah, come off it."

"Yes you did. Before you went out on that thing, there wasn't any oil in the bay. Not a drop. And look at it now."

"The well just blew. No one could help it."

Tina gave her brother a long look that would have withered a bulrush, and concentrated on the sick seabird. She tried to feed it some fish, but it was either not interested or incapable of swallowing.

Craypot was strangely concerned. "I hate seeing innocent things die," he said.

"Perhaps it would help if we bathed him in warm soapy water. It would get rid of the oil."

"Maybe," answered Tina. But Link snorted. "You do that and he'll die for sure. It would take away the natural oils too."

"What would that do?"

"He wouldn't be able to float. He'd drown."

Tina and Craypot both looked so crestfallen that Link felt sorry for them. "In any case," he added, "this fellow is poisoned. Nothing much we can do for him."

"Poisoned?" Tina was horrified.

"Oil poisoning. Swallowed it while he was fishing."

"You mean it's in his stomach and everywhere?"

"Yes. Like a child that's swallowed kerosene."

"Couldn't we make him bring it up? Spit it out?"

"Don't ask me. I'm not a vet."

Craypot was watching the cormorant's eyes. They were closing slowly, as if the eyelids were very tired. "I think he's dying," he said.

Tina was beside herself. "We can't just stand here doing nothing." Then she stopped suddenly. "Mr. Hackett," she said. "He's a scientist. Mr. Hackett will know."

"He knows all right," Craypot said wryly. "He's been spending half his time in the post office, sending telegrams."

Tina dashed for the door of the boat shed, calling to Link.

"Look after him till I get back. Wrap him up warm."

"It's too late," Link called after her. "The thing's dead."

But Tina was already out of earshot, racing across the inlet. She hadn't gone far when she saw Hookie and

Tommy Rough coming around the beach from the headland. They were both carrying seabirds contaminated with oil.

Tina stopped short. "Oh my gosh! More of them!"

Tommy ran forward to meet her. She looked like an attendant at a sump-oil dump, with black streaks across her face and hands, and great splotches over her clothes. She was holding on grimly to a sooty albatross that was still very much alive.

"He can't fly," she panted. "His wings are all gummed up with oil. But the stupid thing doesn't want to be helped."

As she spoke, the albatross wrenched one of its great wings free and started flapping wildly, clouting her loudly on the cheek. By the time she had controlled it she looked like a badly made-up minstrel.

"See what I mean?" she said, through her teeth. "He just won't cooperate."

"He's scared," Tina answered. She stroked the albatross gently. "He doesn't know what's happened to him."

"Mind his beak," Tommy cried, "or you won't know what's happened to you."

Tina grinned. "At least he hasn't slapped my face yet."

Hookie came up then, holding two gulls. They were in a dreadful state, their bright white breasts blackened and polluted, their fine soft feather ends already clogged. "Look at these," he said. "They'll never be able to fly or float properly unless we do something for them."

Tommy gazed back along the way they had come.

"And there'll be more. This is just the start."

Tina nodded. "There'll be hundreds more. Thousands. We've got to hurry." She started to run off, calling to Hookie and Tommy Rough. "Take those three to the boat shed. Link and Craypot will help you with them." Then she raced off around the big sand hill and headed for Mr. Hackett's house.

Luckily Mr. Hackett was at home, working in an enclosed verandah at the back of the house. Tina almost fell forward into the hall when he opened the front door. "Mr. Hackett, the birds . . . all the seabirds . . . are dying. It's because of the . . . of the oil." She gasped it out between breaths, her chest heaving and wheezing from her race up the slope.

"Steady," said Mr. Hackett, ushering her inside. "Good heavens, Tina, slow down or you'll have a heart attack."

But Tina hardly heard him. "It's the oil," she said, "from the well. All the seabirds are getting covered in it. They'll die if they can't get help."

Mr. Hackett looked at her sadly. "I know," he said.

"You do?"

"I've been watching the oil slick since the blowout last Sunday," he said. "I've been measuring it every day and plotting its speed and direction." He looked out through the large front windows of his house toward the sea. "It will reach the coast within a couple of days."

"And the birds?" Tina asked. "Did you know about the birds?"

"Yes; in fact I've been expecting you." He led her through the house to the back lobby where he'd been working. "Look."

Tina's eyes opened in astonishment. There were rows of boxes and cages all along the walls, and in most of them were invalid seabirds of many kinds. Some were lying sick and exhausted, but others were already recovering strongly.

Tina looked at him with admiration. "When did you find them, for goodness' sake?" she asked.

"Yesterday and this morning. Unfortunately it's only the beginning," he said slowly. "We are facing the greatest crisis this part of the coastline has ever seen. That oil slick is still growing, and will continue to grow until the well is controlled. By then it could be ten or fifteen kilometers long. Twenty even."

"But what are we going to do?" Tina said beseechingly. "Whatever in the world are we going to do?"

"We must work hard, and think hard. There are thousands of these fellows in danger—unique creatures, many of them."

"But what?"

"I've made a start," Mr. Hackett said. "I've had a long talk to the Minister for the Environment by telephone. I've told him we must have a boom across the entrance to the bay immediately. And then two or three harbor boats with the latest oil-fighting equipment."

"But it'll come too late. The birds will all be dying by then."

"Many of them will die, Tina; nothing on earth can save them now. But we must try to rescue as many as we can, especially the rarer species. We'll need places where we can keep them until the oil has been cleared away—warm safe places for those that are very sick, and big open places for those that are recovering. We'll need food, lots of it. We'll need helpers, people of all kinds to bring in the victims and look after them—and to bury the ones that die."

Tina looked at him hopelessly. "We'll never do it. There just aren't enough people in Ripple Bay."

"There are a lot," Mr. Hackett said, "especially the children. And there are people who can be leaders, like you, and Link, and Craypot, and . . ."

"Craypot!" Tina snorted. "He wouldn't know whether a tern was a bird or a heart attack."

Mr. Hackett laughed. "You'd be surprised. Craypot has a heart of gold. And he picks things up very quickly."

"Especially when they're dropped by someone else."

Mr. Hackett ignored the comment. "We'll need to mobilize the children from the Area School; the teachers have agreed to come back early from vacation to help organize the rescue teams."

Tina was more and more astonished. "When did you do all that?"

"Yesterday. And last night, on the phone."

"But even then who's going to make all the boxes and line them properly, and find places to put them?"

"Don't worry, reinforcements are on the way."

"What do you mean?"

"We have lots of friends, Tina. At least, the seabirds have."

"What friends?"

"The Ornithologists' Union, Naturalists' Clubs, Conservation Committees. People all over Australia."

"But they won't arrive soon enough. By the time they hear about it and get organized it'll be too late."

"They'll be here this afternoon, many of them. And the rest will arrive tomorrow. Six carloads and a truck loaded with equipment from Melbourne, a busload from Adelaide, even a few from Tasmania."

"Tasmania?"

"Yes. And many of my old colleagues from the University. They're all downing tools or giving up their holidays, to come to Ripple Bay."

Tina was dumbfounded. "How . . . how did they know about it so soon?"

Mr. Hackett smiled at her quizzically.

"Bush telegraph, shall we say."

"Telegrams, that's what. And telephone calls all over the place. Craypot said."

"Craypot shouldn't say. It's not his business."

A new thought struck Tina. "Who's going to pay for it all? Not just the telegrams and that, but the wood and wire for the boxes. And the food. Who's going to pay for all the food?"

Mr. Hackett's smile was broader than ever. "It's all paid for already, every cent of it. As much as we need."

"Who? Not you? Not out of your own pocket?"

"No, much as I'd like to be able to say so. It was someone much richer than I am."

A sudden understanding lit Tina's face. "It was the oil company, wasn't it? Because they are responsible."

Although Mr. Hackett didn't reply, she could see by his expression that she was right. There was a moment's silence. "I'd better be getting back," she said. "There are some very sick patients in the boat shed. One of them's dying."

"There'll be many more," Mr. Hackett said. "We have to concentrate on the ones we can save—especially the fairy penguins."

Tina gave a sudden cry. "Penguins! Oh my gosh! Piglet!"

Mr. Hackett looked at her kindly. "He was all right this morning; he and his mate went out to sea at daybreak." He walked over to the window and gazed out at the huge oil smudge on the water. "Perhaps we should have caught them last night and kept them locked up."

"Yes," said Tina eagerly.

"I was so busy I just didn't think of it."

"Let's do it tonight, then."

He nodded. "I think it would be wise—until the danger is over. Penguins are very very vulnerable."

"Why?"

"Because they can't fly, and because they have to surface frequently to breathe. So they're the first ones to collect the oily muck all over their bodies."

Tina was frightened. "I'll be waiting for Piglet the moment he comes home tonight. I'll keep him safe till the oil has gone."

"Good." Mr. Hackett opened the front door. "I hope I have time to help you."

From that moment on there was barely time to think. Carloads of helpers began to arrive, newspaper reporters and TV cameramen wanted interviews and pictures, and more and more seabirds were being brought in. By the middle of the afternoon it looked as if things were getting out of hand. In the end Mr. Hackett held an urgent meet-

ing with the president of the Royal Australian Ornithologists' Union, who had arrived from Victoria, and they
decided to call everyone together near the boat shed. The
children acted as runners, darting from house to house
with the news until most of the residents and visitors had
been shepherded together into a big assembly outside the
town.

Mr. Hackett was the main speaker. He said a great
crisis was threatening the wildlife of the district. Everyone
could help, but people could do more harm than good if
they didn't know how to go about it. So he was laying
down a few simple rules. "If you see an oiled seabird don't
chase it; use a net or a blanket to catch it, and then put it
into a box gently and quickly." Then he went on with a
list of *don't*s. "Don't wash it, don't use detergents, don't
break its feathers, don't put straw and grass on the floor
of the cages." He followed this with a few clear instructions about what they could do, and then asked for volunteers to act as leaders of special little groups, which he
called task forces and which he was going to send up and
down the coast to keep a constant watch. There were
dozens of people who were willing.

Others were divided into teams to make cages and dis-
tribute food. Mr. Banks gave up all hope of carrying on
his normal work, and virtually handed over the boat shed
to Link and Tina. "All right," he said, "it's yours for a
week. The Bird Cage Construction Corporation."

The visiting helpers put up a big marquee and a lot of
smaller tents among the tussocks on the low-lying ground
behind the boat shed. They brought in trestles and medi-

cal kits, cans of lard and big boxes of rags. And they hung lights all over the place so that they could work at night.

But Tina hardly noticed these things. Long before sunset she was standing high on the headland gazing eagerly out to sea. The weather was calm and the huge oil slick lay on the water like an enormous bruise. Its shoreward edges were very close to the coast now, and she could see only too clearly why Mr. Hackett believed it would reach the rocks and beaches so soon.

Tina stood motionless, her eyes and ears alert for the splash of the returning penguins, or the barking sound of their voices talking to each other a little distance offshore. But there was nothing. Half past eight. Night came down hard and black with only a sliver of moon in the sky, and the air was so still that every slap and ripple of the waves carried up the headland like an echo.

Nine o'clock. Tina still stood unmoving, the fear growing in her heart with every passing minute. Link came looking for her at last, saying that tea was over and Aunt Jessica was in a tizz, but Tina wouldn't budge.

"Something's happened to Piglet," she said hollowly. "I know something has."

Link tried to cheer her up. "He's out late with his girlfriend. There's no need to worry."

"He'd be home by now."

"He'll turn up, you'll see. Come on home."

But she shook her head stubbornly. "I'm going to look for him—up along there."

Link was impatient. "You can't go clumping about at this hour. You'll break your neck. So come on home."

"I'm not coming home till I've found him."

"That's stupid. Have a look in the morning when you can see what you're doing."

"It might be too late, then. He could be lying somewhere, dying. He could be . . ."

There was a catch in her throat and Link knew she couldn't bring herself to say the word "dead." She was close to tears. A wave of pity swept Link. He suddenly felt warmhearted and big-brotherly and sorry for his sister, and so he took her by the elbow and steered her off up the shore. "All right then," he said gently. "We'll both look. I'll come with you."

She gave him a glance of gratitude which, had it been visible in daylight, would probably have made him blush from his armpits to his ears. As it was, they just walked off side by side. They hadn't gone far when they saw a light flashing ahead of them, and presently a dark figure came clomping toward them in seaboots, carrying a bundle. It was Mr. Hackett, with a fairy penguin.

"No, it's not Piglet," he said quickly as Tina rushed forward. "It's a female, poor little thing—and in a bad way."

"Where . . . where did you find her?" Tina asked.

"On the other side of the headland. But there aren't any more that way, not for three or four kilometers anyway."

"Where are they then—Piglet and all the rest? They haven't come home."

"The slick may have frightened them, may have made them roost farther up the coast. Let's hope so anyway."

Mr. Hackett took a fresh grip of the invalid penguin, which lolled weakly against his shoulder like a baby, and squelched off down the shore. "Not much more we can do tonight, Tina," he said. "Better get some sleep and come down again early in the morning."

"Good idea," said Link, steering Tina around and facing her homeward. "We'll be down at first light."

They walked back slowly. As they climbed the headland they could see huge searchlights from *Explorer King* and the support tenders playing on the region of the well.

"They're working around the clock," Link said, "trying to bottle up the blowout."

"Yes," said Tina with sudden passion and bitterness. "Just as they worked around the clock to let it out."

16

By the weekend, Ripple Bay was an unbelievable sight. It had been taken over completely by two huge armies.

At the end of the jetty and spilling out over the reserve and the nearby open ground were the oil commandos led by Indigo Ingvarsson. They were surrounded by such mountains of equipment that the only things they still seemed to lack were cannons and rockets.

On the low ground at the head of the inlet were Mr. Hackett's ecologists and ornithologists, the seabird savers and pollution avengers, who had set up a tent town that swirled around Dave Banks's boat shed, flowed out over the tussocks and dry swampland beyond, and even flapped up the slope toward the bluff. Here and there, on a headland or rocky shore, there was an outrider of this second army—a lookout or a small staging tent.

Between the two warring camps—between the oilmen and the birdmen—there was a small uneasy no-man's-land, which people crossed grimly in silence, as if waiting for gunfire to break out at the first footfall. To some extent the townspeople were caught between these two forces. Although many more supported the ecologists than the oil drillers, they had to try to appear neutral. The hotel had to serve drinks to Mr. Hackett on the one hand and Brenton P. Huxtable on the other; Mrs. Potter's post office had to send off urgent telegrams for both parties; and the bakery and grocery shops sold food to both groups with equal delight and painstakingly equal prices.

Only the fishermen seemed the odd men out. They glowered at the creeping tide of pollution, spat at the water from their boats, and swore at all intruders, no matter where they came from, because they were ruining their livelihood. They also looked sideways at Dave Banks, because he and old *Titan* had been hired for yet one more outlandish job. This time it was for the Department of Marine and Harbours—to help put a boom across the entrance of the bay in a last-ditch attempt to keep the oil sludge away from the town.

By Saturday Link felt a sense of claustrophobia, as if Ripple Bay was being crushed to death by people. And there were rumors of even more to come—technicians, engineers, oil experts, geologists—to watch Indigo Ingvarsson's battle with Albatross Two, and to make decisions about the future. For the accuracy that was needed was unbelievable—to drill a curving well, bent like a banana, so perfectly that it would intersect a narrow hole thousands of meters below the floor of the sea.

"I don't see how they can do it," Link said flatly when Bob Joy first told him about it. "It would be like trying to skewer a worm deep under your lawn with a ten-meter needle."

"They can do it all right," Bob answered; "especially with computers and electronics. Right on the button."

"Have they ever done it before?"

"Dozens of times. It's meat and drink to fellows like Indigo."

"But how long is it going to take?"

"Not all that long. They're using *Explorer King* and they're well on the way down already—drilling like crazy, day and night, with high-speed bits and no money spared. They'll control old bellow-guts out there, no worries. Snuff it out like a candle from below."

"I hope you're right," Link said. "And they'd better hurry."

On Saturday morning the oil slick reached the northwest coast beyond the town, just as Mr. Hackett had predicted. The oil gave a greasy sheen to the waves as they arched over and broke. But instead of shattering into crisp white water, they surged over the rocks in a dark sludge, soiling everything they touched. Before long the pebbles and sand, the sharp white shells, the bits of cuttlefish, and all the fragments of the sea's bright bric-a-brac were smeared and evil smelling.

The poisonous ripples ran in under the boulders, probed into the cracks and fissures like slippery gloved fingers, brought stench and destruction into the most secret places. They flowed into the rock pools and left behind a reeking scum; they invaded the rarest grottoes and left them fouled in an instant. Wherever the dark tide flowed it destroyed life. Fish, cockle and crab, crayfish and mussel, sea snail and urchin—for each equally the taint of oil was the taint of death. Happily, to the southeast the creeping sludge still hung a kilometer from the coast, but its movement was relentlessly shoreward and it was only a matter of time before there, too, its suffocating reach would embrace the rocky beaches and snuff out the life that was there.

Through it all, Tina's ceaseless search for Piglet went on. All day Friday, far into Friday night, and all day Saturday she roamed the shoreline to the north and south. In the darkness before dawn, and in the twilight after sunset, she waited near his little burrow, calling his name, listening for his skitter and splash. But there was no response, no sound, nothing. She was a forlorn sight among the press of rescuers. Whenever there was news of another fairy penguin being found—whether dead, dying, or alive—she rushed to the place where it had been brought in. But it was never Piglet.

People commented about her and pitied her; Link tried to help her; Mr. Hackett tried to comfort her amid the turmoil of his other tasks. But she remained stubbornly aloof, tense and alert, driving herself on, until she was ready to drop.

Saturday evening was beginning to close in and she was on her way back from the far headland to take up her vigil by the rookery again. She was with Craypot. Not that she particularly wanted to be with anyone, but Link had been called away to help his father on the harbor boom and Craypot had taken his place beside Tina of his own accord. Most of the other workers were gathering around the tents to help feed the rescued birds or prepare their own meals.

Tina and Craypot were picking their way among the fallen boulders at the foot of the cliffs. They were both dog tired and their feet were slipping and stumbling. The evening shadows were deepening rapidly too, and it was hard to see the outlines of things clearly.

Suddenly Tina stopped and stood listening tensely. Craypot, who was close behind, blundered into her and took a moment to recover.

"Listen." Tina was trembling, her senses taut. "Did you hear anything?" She made a soft clicking noise with her tongue and started calling softly. "Piglet! Piglet! Is that you, Piglet?"

Craypot was all atingle too. Although he was peering urgently in every direction, he couldn't make out a thing in the gloom. He was about to take a step forward when he heard a faint, queer sound—half squeak, half gurgle—followed by a flopping, slipping noise in the rocks to the left. At the same time Tina gave a cry and leaped forward, sliding and groveling about among the oil-coated stones and fissures. "Piglet," she called. "Where are you? Where are you?" And then, suddenly, they both saw him. He was lying between two big stones near the cliff face, covered with muck and oil, so much like a stone himself that they could barely distinguish him from his surroundings. As Tina clambered desperately toward him he managed to stand up, but he was very weak and the greasy ooze around him was so slippery that he couldn't keep a foothold, so he flopped down pathetically on his back, just as Tina reached him.

She picked him up gently, and held him against her chest. "Piglet! Oh, Piglet." There was no doubt whatever that it was Piglet. Apart from the disk on his flipper. Tina could tell instinctively by the way the little penguin tried to nuzzle into her shoulder. And by the funny crooning noise of recognition and happiness he made at the back of his throat. Tina knelt there like someone in prayer, rocking

him as gently as a baby. "Oh Piglet! You poor, poor fellow."
Craypot stood by while Tina got up unsteadily, clutching
the penguin, and made her way back to where he was waiting. He held out his hand to steady her.

"Just look at him!" she said. "He's soaked through and
through with it."

Craypot felt Piglet's feathers and peered at him closely.
"D'you think that he'll . . . well, that he'll be all right?"

Tina looked at him sharply, but his very question seemed
to spur her on. "We must hurry," she said, walking a little
breathlessly. "I'll take him straight to Mr. Hackett."

They reached the tumbledown track up the cliff and
climbed carefully to the top. Three or four times Craypot
had to support Tina, who couldn't get a handhold because
she was nursing Piglet. But in the end they made it, staggering about like exhausted mountain climbers, and headed
straight for Mr. Hackett's house.

Luckily he was at home. He, too, was so drawn with ex-
haustion that he was almost bowled over by Tina's headlong rush when he opened the door.

"We've found him! We've found him!" she said. "And
he's alive."

Mr. Hackett recovered and glanced quickly at Piglet
lying limp in her arms.

"Only just," he said. "Only just."

He hurried them into the lobby, where they laid Piglet
gently on the bench. He was a terrible sight. There was not
a spot on his body that wasn't tacky with oil and scum. Mr.
Hackett examined him quickly. "Poor old Piglet," he said.
"You're in a bad way." He turned to Tina. "We'll have to

hurry. He's suffering from all the effects of oil pollution—shock, cold, feather damage, poisoning. And he's probably half starved." He bustled about with a large bundle of woollen rag. "We're lucky that he knows us, so he won't waste his energy in useless struggling." He gave some of the rag to Tina and Craypot. "Remove what oil you can. But do it carefully. Always stroke downward to avoid breaking or damaging the feathers."

They worked silently and breathlessly. As they cleaned the muck from his head and throat, he blinked his eyes fast and wriggled for a minute, but he soon settled down as they wiped the rest of his body.

"Now," said Mr. Hackett, hurrying up with a large can and several bottles. "Smear him well with lard."

Tina looked up quickly, wrinkling her face in distaste. "With *lard*? Just when we're starting to clean him up a bit?"

"Yes, lard. And a bit of maize or peanut oil. Any animal or vegetable fats."

Tina turned to do as she was told. "Sorry Piglet," she whispered, "but it's for your own good."

"Then dust some fuller's earth into his feathers. It's in that tin. To absorb the excess fat and oil."

For the most part the little penguin lay on the bench like a pathetic bundle while they worked on him. He was plainly too weak to struggle much, even if he had wanted to.

Mr. Hackett looked at him closely. "We mustn't handle him too much," he said. "He has to rest in a warm, quiet place."

Craypot picked up a large empty box from he bench. "Shall we put him in here?"

"Not yet. We'll give him a dose of cod-liver oil to relieve the internal irritation." He seized a dessertspoon and filled it from a bottle on the shelf. "Hold him up, Tina. That's it." And he poured the cod-liver oil down Piglet's throat before he knew what was happening.

"Is that all?" asked Tina.

"We'll just try him on food. If he vomits, or hemorrhages, or refuses to eat, he's probably badly poisoned."

Mr. Hackett took a small pilchard from a bucket and dipped it thoroughly in water. "Now, Tina. Hold him up firmly and carefully." Then he took Piglet's bill, pried it open gently, and pushed the fish headfirst well down into the back of his throat. Piglet struggled for a second, but then he arched his neck and swallowed the pilchard at a gulp. They all watched to see if he was going to regurgitate it. But nothing happened.

"Good," said Mr. Hackett. "Very good."

Tina looked up at him, her eyes bright with hope. "He is going to be all right, isn't he?"

Mr. Hackett was silent.

"Isn't he?" Tina said it more insistently, with just a trace of alarm in her voice.

Mr. Hackett didn't answer directly. "Now, put plenty of soft woollen rag on the bottom of the box. No loose ends or threads for him to get tangled in. That's right. And then put him inside carefully and bring him into the spare bedroom where he can be kept warm and undisturbed."

Craypot carried the box inside and put it in a quiet corner. Then they went into the living room, leaving the door half closed. Tina and Craypot suddenly realized that they were walking on tiptoe.

Mr. Hackett wiped his hands and wrinkled his nose. "I smell like a fish shop," he said. "Worse than that. Pilchards, cormorants, penguins, silver gulls, albatrosses—and oil. What a combination." Then he turned to Tina. "About Piglet. I can't say. He's very sick. We don't know how long he's been like that, how much body heat he's lost, or how much oil he's swallowed." He paused. "But I'll say this. If he's no worse in the morning, he should have a fifty-fifty chance of pulling through."

Tina was clenching and unclenching her hands, unaware that she was doing it. "He'll be all right. I know he will."

Mr. Hackett opened his mouth as if to sound a warning that many other penguins like Piglet had already died, but he thought better of it.

"Let's hope so," he said. "Let's all hope so."

But Piglet was no better in the morning. If anything, he was worse. He lay limply on his side with his eyes closed most of the time, taking no interest in food or drink. Tina, who had come racing up hopefully to Mr. Hackett's house at the crack of dawn, was near tears when she saw him. "What can we do?" she kept asking Mr. Hackett over and over. "Whatever can we do?"

"We've done all we can for the moment," he answered, shifting a heater a little closer to Piglet's box to keep him warm. "This is a battle he has to fight on his own now. We call it the will to live."

227

"Piglet has got it; I'm sure he has," she said doggedly.

But when she looked at the sad little bundle lying in the box she was far from sure. In her heart she was frightened at what might happen, at what might be happening already. And at the terrible helplessness of everybody, even Mr. Hackett.

Craypot came in from his house next door, full of pity and concern, but there was nothing he could do either. He and Tina knelt over Piglet's box, one on either side, so motionless and silent that they looked like a couple of carved bookends pushed together. The tops of their heads collided for a moment and, when they both looked up quickly, Craypot's nose poked Tina in the eye. She almost laughed and a warm feeling of regard for Craypot and his kindness swept over her. Impulsively, she stood up and took his hand as naturally as if he had been Link or her father.

"Come out and help Mr. Hackett with breakfast," she said.

But when they reached the kitchen, Mr. Hackett had already finished and was on the point of setting off for the beach.

"Leave Piglet for an hour or two," he said. "He's safe and warm where he is, and there's nothing more we can do for him now. We'll see how he is at lunchtime. Meanwhile there's plenty for us to do down at the camp."

They walked off side by side under the wide morning. Halfway down they met a group of helpers from the camp and stopped short. They were carrying three big laundry baskets among them, each one piled high with dead birds.

Mr. Hackett looked quickly at Tina. She was staring at them aghast.

"Last night's crop," one of the men said brutally. "Either dead on the shore this morning or died in the compounds overnight."

"On your way to bury them?" Mr. Hackett asked.

"Yes. Up the sand hill."

"Mixed lot."

"Something of everything. Penguins as usual. They cop it. Poor fellows."

Tina couldn't take her eyes off the three big baskets overflowing with death. There was something terribly callous about the way the dead birds lay tumbled together stiffly in angles and attitudes, beaks protruding dumbly over the edges, wings sticking lifelessly upward like feathered boards, claws clenched hard. All the grace and beauty of their flight lay locked there and lost forever.

"We'd better get busy," the man said. "Need a big trench, this lot." And he picked up his shovel and led his carriers slowly up the slope. To Tina they looked like ghouls.

Craypot nudged Tina gently. "Let's go," he said.

At the camp the morning's work was in full swing— feeding, drying, cleaning, swabbing, brushing, preening, coaxing, scolding. Mr. Hackett was soon caught up with lots of questions and problems, so Tina and Craypot slipped off to lend the other rescuers a hand. Several hours went by, hours filled with squawking beaks and flapping wings, and with joy, sadness, and exasperation. But it was all over for the morning at last, and they washed their hands in the basin in the boat shed. As they walked back afterward, they unexpectedly came upon a large group of people gathered together in an open space between the tents.

"What's up?" Tina asked. "Not another argument with the fishermen?"

"Don't be nitty," Craypot laughed. "It's a church service. It's Sunday morning, remember?"

"A church service? Out here?"

"What's wrong with that?"

"Seems queer, that's all."

"People often have them outside. Weddings, celebrations, all sorts of ceremonies."

They stood watching near a tent at the back of the congregation. When the first hymn was announced, the sound of the singing rose up so roundly and clearly that it seemed to fill the morning. High white clouds and warm sunshine, a still town and a soft horizon, a breeze in the tent flaps, and friendly old tussocks underfoot, and over everything the sound of the voices singing—it was all strangely beautiful. But then the breeze strengthened and there was oil on its breath, a hard, acrid kind of smell that irritated their nostrils and hung on the air around them. And for Tina it immediately brought pictures of a little penguin lying limply in a box in Mr. Hackett's bedroom, fighting for its life.

The minister was speaking now in a loud ringing voice, reading the lesson for the day. It urged people to give thanks for all the beautiful things around them, and for all the world's goodness and wonder.

Tina looked at Craypot, who was looking at the ground —perhaps because he went to church more often than she did and because his mother frowned on people who gawked about all over the place during the service. She lifted her eyes to the people, and to the minister standing upright with a white Bible in his hands, and to the far horizon beyond his head. For a fleeting second he dissolved into another minister, long ago, standing like that during the funeral ceremony of a woman who had drowned.

"Let us pray," said the minister, and the people in the congregation bowed their heads, kneeling simply on the dry tussocks and grass. The minister talked his prayer aloud to God, asking for many things, and many forgivenesses, and much help. And especially for pity and succor for the town and its people, and for the wild creatures of the sea and air. As she listened, Tina again saw a little penguin in her mind's eye, lying helplessly and desperately ill. She closed her eyes and turned her face toward the high morning light and the feel of the warm sunshine.

"And, dear God," she said softly and quickly to herself, "please let Piglet live. Please let him live." Half a sob gathered in her throat and she fought to keep it from rising; but then tears began to form behind her closed eyelids and no matter how hard she pressed, they squeezed their way out and dribbled between her lashes. She lowered her head quickly so that they could drop off straight into the grass instead of leaving wet telltale channels down her cheeks.

Craypot knew what was happening and trembled with the urge to put his arm around her and comfort her, but he was convinced that anyone who saw him would not understand or approve.

After a while Tina began searching up her sleeves for a

handkerchief. When she failed to find one, she drew in her breath in long watery sniffs and wiped her arm across her eyes slowly and deliberately. Then she turned and retreated silently behind the line of tents. Craypot followed her.

"Why didn't you stay to the end?" he asked.

"Couldn't stand it any longer," she answered, her voice quavering a little, despite her efforts to steady it, and her lashes still moist. "I'm going up to watch over Piglet."

Craypot understood.

"I'll come with you," he said.

17

On Sunday afternoon Link and his father finally came ashore. They were dead beat. Both had been battling without rest to finish the harbor boom, but though they had reinforced the long line of pine trunks and floating drums, and laced the framework with brush and bracken, some of the oil had begun to seep through. Nevertheless they had done their best and had kept most of the creeping black tide away from the foreshore.

They were talking to Tina and Mr. Hackett, and a few of their friends near the boat shed, when Bob Joy's helicopter chattered overhead with a flirt of its tail and landed cheekily nearby. The bubble doors had hardly opened when Brenton P. Huxtable and Indigo Ingvarsson stepped out. Both looked tired, but Mr. Huxtable held his arm out in greeting long before he was near enough to attach it to anyone.

"How are you, Dave?" he called, striding toward Link's father. "Been doing a mighty fine job on that there boom. Been watching you, man." He turned to Link. "And you too, Link. Good work, boy." He turned to the whole group and stood beaming. "Well, folks," he said in the manner of a great announcement, "we're bringing you all good news. That old spitfire out there should be dead within a week. Yes sir. After Saturday I reckon you ain't gonna have no more trouble out of that cannon mouth. No sir." He seized Indigo by the arm and propelled him forward. "And this is the guy to thank, folks. Indigo K. Ingvarsson. Hot-shot Indigo, to his friends. The computer says he's right on the button as usual. Beautiful drilling, yes sir."

Indigo said only one or two words; then he excused himself and went off to organize men and machinery near the jetty. It wasn't until much later that the full story of his work came out simply and clearly; that he had driven crews and machinery to breaking point, until his offset well had cut into Albatross Two deep near its source. Then tons and tons of heavy mud had slowly quelled the hideous uprush of gas and oil, squeezing into the fractured formations, sealing the subsidiary blowouts in the strata all around, and finally building up into a gigantic plug that silenced the well's rampage and quenched its inferno forever.

At first, Brenton P. Huxtable wanted to buy everyone a drink, but when he discovered that the hotel bars were closed and his guests were lukewarm, he gave up the idea. Finally, when Mr. Hackett remarked ironically that the town would have something to remember him by in any case, he excused himself and went to help Indigo.

"Lots of things to do," he said urgently. "Got to get ready to spud in a new well, couple of kilometers southeast. Albatross Two might have been a fire-breathing old son of a bitch, but she sure led us to the treasure, yes sir."

Mr. Hackett suddenly sighed deeply and loudly. Then he turned and went back to the tents.

Tina was flushed and angry. "D'you mean you're going

to drill another well, after all the death and destruction this one has caused?"

"Just as soon as we can. We've lost a million dollars on this crazy blowhard, so we have to get that back. Yes sir."

He could see the anger so clearly in her eyes that he paused. When he spoke again, it was on a different tack. "What's more, you and your people need that oil real bad. You sure do."

Tina's face reddened and Link thought she was about to sound off in a fury. But she seemed to check herself at the last minute. "Ah what's the use!" she said bitterly. Then she turned and followed Mr. Hackett.

Anxious to restore its public image, the oil company used all its resources to help with the huge cleanup. It converted the empty mud-pods on one of its tenders into detergent tanks and sprayed the whole of the oil slick with its high-pressure pumps to break up the surface oil. The Government had already sent an antipollution team with land-based tankers to spray the rocks and the beaches.

"Within a week," Mr. Brenton P. Huxtable said heartily to Mrs. Potter at the counter of the post office, "we will have pulled out of Ripple Bay completely—supplies, equipment, the lot. Indigo will be back in the States, and old *Explorer King* will be down on the horizon sitting over a brand-new hole." He smiled at her expansively. "You won't even know that we've been here."

But, like Tina and Mr. Hackett, Craypot's mother gave him a withering look and stalked coldly away.

Tina went back up the bluff to Mr. Hackett's house and

sat watching Piglet for a long time. Sometimes, when he opened his eyes and peered at her in something of his old inquisitive way, she felt a great surge of happiness and hope. She leaned forward, stroked his poor bedraggled body, and spoke to him quietly and soothingly. But sometimes, when he lay limp and unmoving for long periods with his eyes closed, all her fears returned.

Once or twice she thought she heard voices and the sound of distant shouting, but she didn't move. It wasn't until footsteps came clumping up to the front gate that she got up wearily and went to the door. It was Mr. Hackett with Link, Craypot, and her father.

"How's the patient?" Mr. Hackett asked.

"The same, I think. Sometimes he seems a bit better and sometimes he's worse."

"As long as he's holding his own." He went out to the kitchen and put on the kettle.

"We've come home for a cleanup and a pot of tea."

Mr. Banks stood at the window, gazing down at the reserve near the jetty. He chuckled quietly. "Did you hear the commotion a while ago?" he asked.

Tina tried to remember. "Oh yes, there was a noise of some sort."

Link and Craypot laughed out loud. "Some noise. I reckon they would have heard it on the other side of Bass Strait."

"Why, what happened?"

Craypot was hugging himself with delight. "The fishermen marched on the oil company. Put pickets around all their gear—cement, barite, scientific equipment, supplies. Even the helicopters."

Tina looked at him blankly. "What sort of pickets?"

Link gestured impatiently. "Ah come on Tina. Wakey! Wakey!"

"Fence pickets?"

"Human pickets, dill sister! Union men, workmates, fellow fishermen."

Tina understood, but pulled a sour face at her brother for his rudeness—especially in front of Craypot.

Luckily Craypot was even more excited by what the fishermen had done than Link was.

"It was fantastic," he said gleefully. "There were all these fellows standing in a great wide circle around the oil company's depot. Mr. Huxtable came down with Indigo Ingvarsson and Bob Joy to get into the helicopter, and when the fishermen wouldn't let them through, he drew himself up tall and said, 'We've got to get to Melbourne tonight, so just stand aside.' Then it was on."

Tina was beginning to feel sorry she'd missed it all. "What happened?"

"What didn't happen?" said Mr. Hackett, returning from the kitchen. "It was just like a football match—Mario shouting his head off, John Leckie threatening to punch Mr. Huxtable on the nose, Steve Hanson urging someone to cut off the rotor blades from the helicopter . . ."

"Picnic party," added Mr. Banks laconically.

Craypot laughed. "But they settled it in the end."

"How?"

"Indigo Ingvarsson refused to waste any more time."

"What did he do?"

"He just said, 'Give the men what they want!' Just like that."

"And what did they want?"

"Compensation for lost livelihood—for all the fish they say they've missed because of the oil spill."

"That would add up to a fair bit."

"No worries. The company agreed to pay."

"Fair enough, too," said Mr. Hackett, coming in with the teapot.

Link hadn't said much. His mind was a turmoil of conflict—at one minute full of sympathy for the fishermen, at the next torn and anguished over the lost oil well and the whole sad story of Albatross Two.

Mr. Huxtable was right about the offset hole. It took exactly one more week to quell the well completely. But there were no cheers and celebrations on shore. As far as the townspeople were concerned, it was a battle by remote control, a grim scientific struggle that went on thousands of meters below the sea, far beyond their world. They lived with the effects, not with the causes: with oil slicks, ruined fishing grounds, and dying seabirds, not with Cretaceous graywackes and abnormal fault zones. And so, when the oil company at last made an announcement declaring that Albatross Two was officially sealed and dead, everyone merely muttered a private thanks and went on with the job of clearing up.

Piglet had hung on desperately to his spark of life for the whole week. Sometimes Mr. Hackett despaired silently when Tina was not about, and sometimes he was gently confident. But he was never really sure.

On Sunday afternoon he invited his friends for a cup

of tea, as he had the week before. They all seemed many weeks older and wiser. "My poor old bones," Mr. Hackett said. "The end of that well hasn't come any too soon; we've still got some tough days ahead, but I think we're over the hill."

Mr. Banks was standing by the window again. "Look," he said, pointing. "The rig's on the move."

They all crowded forward, gazing. "So it is."

Mr. Hackett suddenly nudged them all impulsively. "Come out to the headland," he said. "I'd rather like to see it off."

Craypot reluctantly excused himself because he had promised to help his mother, but the others agreed. The wind was rising from the south and a slop was running against the rugged shoreline. The reek of oil still hung heavily on the air. They sat down on the rocks at the cliff edge above Piglet's old home and gazed out to sea. The superstructure of *Explorer King* was still visible, but it was low on the horizon and moving steadily southeastward.

"So it's going at last," Mr. Banks said. "It really is going."

Tina set her mouth in a hard line. "Good riddance. It's nothing but a juggernaut."

Link said nothing. He sat with his knees up under his chin, gazing at the great rig inching down into the sea haze. Wrapped in his own daydream he could hear The Sausage's words clearly in his ears. "Any time you want a job, Link, I take you back. No worries." It had been exciting, that job on the rig. If he had the chance, he'd do it again. For a minute the whole incredible scene came back vividly before his eyes—the drilling table and the draw works, the crown block and the kelly, the slips and the tongs. And the whole gallery of crewmen: Hank, the tool pusher, and Eddie; The Sausage and The Barrel; Bob Joy in his helicopter; and Andy Freeman sitting among his geological specimens in the laboratory. And Mr. Brenton P. Huxtable.

"We won't forget her in a hurry," Mr. Hackett said. "Town changed forever, shoreline ruined, half the penguins dead . . . and God knows what it's done to the crayfishing industry."

They were all silent for a while in their own worlds. Tina was thinking of Piglet's mate, who had never returned, and of Piglet himself, still hovering between life and death. Link was wondering which team would take the first drilling shift, and whether the new well would be called Albatross Three. Mr. Banks was trying to decide whether to expand his boat shed to cope with increased business if the town grew.

"I'm glad to see the end of it," Tina said. "It brought nothing but trouble."

"But it's not the end of it, Tina. It's just the beginning," Mr. Hackett replied. "People know that there's oil and gas there now. Lots of it. They won't rest until they get it."

"Why can't they just leave it where it is and forget about it? Last year they didn't know it was there, but things went on just the same."

Mr. Hackett gazed across the water at the faint smudge of *Explorer King*. "The world doesn't work that way. Man is a busy animal, far too acquisitive and ruthless to do a thing like that. It would be like walking backward."

"So we ruin everything."

"From one point of view, no. We're concerned about trade and transport, about fuel for fast cars, about heating and cooking, and comfort in our houses; about what we call standard of living."

"So they'll drill a new well."

"Not just one. Dozens. Hundreds maybe. Pipelines will snake about under the sea like boa constrictors, bringing the gas and oil ashore. There'll be tank farms right here where we're sitting, and pumping stations and purifying plants as well. The bay will be deepened and widened, the swamp filled in, and thousands of people will come to live and work in the town. There'll be roadhouses, and neon signs, and motels, and motor bikes, and a civic center, and public lavatories."

"And no penguins."

"And no penguins."

Mr. Hackett stood up. He looked toward the inlet where some of the helpers were pulling down their tents and packing up. "I'd better go down and lend a hand," he said. "Many of them have to be back at work tomorrow."

Mr. Banks stood up too. "That's right, it'll be Monday morning. I've lost all track of time."

Link pulled a wry face. "Back to school," he said.

Tina set her jaw stubbornly. "I'm not going; not till we know whether . . . till we know about Piglet."

Her father eyed her sharply, but said nothing. Instead

he turned to Mr. Hackett, as they all began walking down from the bluff. "I guess you'll have plenty to keep yourself busy for a while—especially without your helpers."

"For a week or two, yes. But things will gradually sort themselves out."

"Then what? A holiday?"

"Then I think I'll pack up too. Move on somewhere else."

They all stopped short. "Oh no!" Tina cried. "You're not leaving Ripple Bay?"

He looked at her gently, and nodded. "I'm afraid so, Tina. There's no wildlife left here for me to study, now."

"Where will you go?" Mr. Banks asked. "The last frontier? It's getting hard to find."

"Yes. But I'm sure there's still a lonely seashore somewhere. Perhaps on the West Coast. With a mailman going past once a week, and no cars. Not even any electricity."

"Just lamps."

"Just lamps."

"You'll need oil for them, of course," said Mr. Banks; "but you can buy that from the oil companies."

Mr. Hackett laughed heartily at the joke against himself.

"I'll get it from Ripple Bay," he said.

"No, we'll send you some candles."

Tina and Link walked side by side a little distance apart from the two men. They didn't speak, but each knew what was in the other's heart. Ever since their mother had died, they had always come together strangely like this in time of loss and crisis. The rising wind off the sea was chill-fingered on their cheeks, but it carried something more than physical cold.

"It won't be the same," Mr. Banks said.

"It certainly won't." Mr. Hackett looked keenly at Tina and Link. "When an hour or even a minute passes, nothing can ever be the same again."

Format by Gloria Bressler
Set in 11 pt. Baskerville
Composed, printed and bound by The Haddon Craftsmen, Inc.
HARPER & ROW, PUBLISHERS, INCORPORATED